High Plains Holiday

LOVE ON THE HIGH PLAINS BOOK 1

SIMONE BEAUDELAIRE

This book is dedicated to the people of Garden City, Kansas. It was a wonderful place to live.
I would like to thank those who helped me prepare this novel for publication, my wonderful beta readers Sandra Martinez, Lisa Williamson, and James DiBenedetto. Thank you all.

Prologue

GARDEN CITY, KS 1873

K ristina Heitschmidt hurried north along the rutted wagon tracks beyond the edge of town, where an abandoned soddie doubled as a hideout and clubhouse.

I'm so late, she fretted, noting the position of the sun high overhead. *I'm always late these days. Jesse's sure to tease.*

In the last year or so, she'd been unable to drag herself away from the piano and out to play. Allison, her best friend, also took piano lessons, but unlike Kristina, she saw the hours spent slaving on the instrument as a waste of time. Time that could be better spent playing train robbers or cowboys and Indians with Jesse and Wesley.

Last year, I felt the same way, but that was before the new pastor came to town.

Reverend Miller's wife—an accomplished pianist and organist —began teaching the children music. Only Kristina really seemed to take to it though. A year later, her enthusiasm hadn't waned a bit.

Beside the remains of a decaying barn, an odd shape loomed on the horizon. It looked like half a massive barrel sunk deep into

1

the soil, the prairie grass growing on the surface. The front door had long since fallen in, and it gaped like an open mouth.

Kristina shuddered, even though she knew the interior would be cool on a hot summer's day. A fat black spider scuttled up the doorjamb. *Ugh. Be brave. They already think you're a baby. Don't act like one too.*

She hurried inside and squealed as Jesse grabbed her, yanking her to one side and shoving a pistol made from a bit of bent lead pipe against her temple.

"Kristina!" Allison shrieked, pulling a black bandana down from her face. Her blue eyes sparkled with the fun of the game.

"Stop or I shoot," Jesse hollered, attempting to tip back his oversized hat and accidentally knocking it to the dirt floor of the pioneer home. Kristina heard the soft thump as it landed. Now, she knew, his yellow hair would shine like a beacon in the dimness of the room.

"Let her go," Wesley said in a soft, authoritative voice, stepping carefully into the room in a pair of oversized spurs. One caught on the threshold, and he stumbled, falling into Jesse and knocking the smaller boy off balance. The bit of pipe jammed into Kristina's temple with bruising force as the three of them went down in a heap.

"Owwww," Kristina whined, clutching the side of her head.

"Aw, stop crying, you baby," Jesse replied curtly.

"I'm going to have a big bruise," Kristina accused, "and it's all your fault."

"All Wes's, you mean," he protested. "He fell, not me. Besides, with all those spots on your face, no one will notice."

"Shut up," Kristina said, uttering the foulest word any of them knew. She stuck out a trembling lip.

Wesley sighed in disgust. "A baby *and* a girl. Maybe you shouldn't play with us anymore."

"Nuh-uh Allison protested. "Kristina is my *best friend*. If she doesn't play, neither do I. Are you okay, Kris?"

"I guess," Kristina sulked.

"I thought *I* was your best friend," Wesley said, sounding hurt. He pulled himself from the tangle of limbs, accidentally poking Jesse in the arm with one of the spurs.

"Hey, be careful," the boy protested.

"You are my best friend," Allison replied. "You all are. The four of us will be friends forever."

Chapter One

GARDEN CITY, KS 1888

"And last but not least, the church." James Heitschmidt waved a hand towards the steepled structure.

Big church for such a small town, Reverend Cody Williams thought. His gaze traveled up the façade, from the thick stone foundation to the tip of the steeple, where a gleaming wooden cross crowned an open-sided bell tower with a hefty bell visible from the street.

Lower down, above the arched doorway, a round stained-glass window bore an image of a green hill, on which three crosses strained towards a blue sky. It was simply rendered but no less lovely because of it.

A gust of icy wind shot down the street and straight through the young man's thin wool coat into his flesh, chilling him deep. After five years in Galveston's soupy heat, this cold, blustery town would take some getting used to.

Cody mounted the groaning wooden steps and reached for the handle of one of the peaked doors. At that moment, a blast of sound so loud it nearly sent him tumbling on his back reverberated through the building. The low, rumbling vibration made his eardrums feel expanded, as though he had dived deep underwater.

The tone was followed by another, a little higher, and then a third before being replaced by a lilting melody. Now Cody recognized the tune from his required music classes at seminary. "All My Heart This Night Rejoices" by Johann Sebastian Bach.

Recovering his balance and composure, Cody grasped the wrought-iron handle and hissed as the frigid metal burned his bare hand. *I need gloves as soon as possible. Of course, I'll have to wait until I begin earning a salary first. I wonder how much they'll pay me. The letters said 'a comfortable living wage,' but who knows what that means.*

He stepped over the high threshold, making a mental note not to stumble on it.

James followed, closing the door behind him.

The weak November sunshine barely penetrated the stained-glass windows that lined each of the two longer interior walls. One side featured six scenes from the Old Testament: The Garden of Eden, Noah's Ark, the Ten Commandments, the walls of Jericho, David and Goliath, and finally, Elijah taking on the prophets of Baal while stones and water burned.

Cody glanced across the room to the other side. Just as he suspected, a Nativity Scene, the boy Jesus at the temple, Jesus turning water into wine, the healing of the blind man, a crucifixion, and the scene of the empty tomb. All of Christian faith summed up in twelve simple, crudely-rendered collections of glass and lead. They were far from works of art, but Cody preferred their simplicity. They felt more real this way, something everyday folk could understand.

The organist finished the piece and immediately launched into a lively rendition of "Joy to the World." The rumbling bass of the foot pedals kept time while fingers plunked out a rolling counterpoint. Cody heard a soft thump as the musician changed the stops, and the new verse had a different quality than the previous one.

From his spot at the back of the church, Cody couldn't see the organ. It stood on a balcony directly above him, but the pipes wrapped around the upper walls to the front, behind his pulpit. *Seems odd that a church in such a small town would have such a magnificent organ. Perhaps it was built specifically for this musician. If so, it was worth the exorbitant cost. I hope the man isn't too high-strung.*

On either side of the aisle stretched row after row of gleaming wooden pews, each with a scarlet cushion running its entire length. Ornate patterns of vines and leaves scrolled on the wooden arms.

Darker than the pews, the wooden floor shone in a high polish. At the front, a long communion rail with delicate spindles curved around the single step, split in the center by his pulpit. Before each one lay another cushion, also deep red, for people to kneel on while receiving the bread and wine. A potbellied stove in the rear corner provided heat.

Sharp contrast drew his eyes to the ceiling. Adorning the whitewashed boards, mahogany beams crossed each other over and over.

Cody regarded the pulpit again. Unlike the rest of the church, the plain, unadorned brown box for him to set his notes on suited him fine. He felt no need for displays of extravagance.

The song ended, and James boomed out, "Stop practicing now, Kristina, and come down here. There's someone I want you to meet." His Kansas twang still sounded strange to Cody, who had lived his whole life in Texas. Then the words registered.

Kristina? But... that's a woman's name. Who is Kristina and where is she? Why is James calling her?

A clatter of high-heeled boots drew Cody's gaze to the steps, and he turned to see those boots appearing at the top of the twisting staircase. Flashes of dove gray leather, almost hidden under a skirt of the same color, covered a figure that nipped in sharply at the middle, before swelling again to fill a white shirtwaist, buttoned to the neck and covered with a black crocheted shawl.

At last, he could see the face, and his own went slack with astonishment. Her braided bun was gold, not silver. It gleamed with hints of red, even in the weak sunlight. The face, though smooth and unlined, made his smile fade.

Kristina was not a lovely girl. Heavy freckles dotted every inch of her skin. Adding a short, upturned nose and a firm, stubborn jaw, she resembled a brindled bulldog.

On the other hand, her eyes sparkled with turquoise warmth, like the Gulf of Mexico, and her full, pink slips curved into a perfect Cupid's bow.

"Reverend Williams, this is my daughter, Kristina Heitschmidt. Kristina, this is our new pastor, Reverend Cody Williams."

Kristina gave him a frank, appraising look and extended her hand. He grasped it. She wore no gloves, and her fingers felt nearly as cold as his.

"Pleased to meet you, Miss Heitschmidt," he drawled, wondering how his Texas accent would sound to them.

"Likewise, Reverend. We've heard so much about you." She smiled, and her face changed from bulldog to appealing puppy. He couldn't help but smile back. "Dad," Kristina scolded, "you never told me Reverend Williams was so young and handsome. All the young ladies will be chasing him."

Cody colored at the unexpected compliment. He knew he was not a bad-looking man. The mirror this morning had shown black hair with a hint of a curl, bright blue eyes, smooth skin. Nothing so handsome as to cause jealousy, or so he hoped. Being chased by a bunch of silly young girls would be a nuisance and a distraction. "Was that you playing the organ?"

"Yes," she replied, lowering her burnished gold eyebrows. The movement caused her short nose to wrinkle.

Something about this woman made him feel slightly off-balance, as though he couldn't draw a full breath. He blurted. "Where did you learn to play like that?"

She smiled, though it didn't look altogether convincing. "From the previous pastor's wife. She had no children, so she sort of adopted me when I was six, taught me piano, organ, and voice."

"Excellent. Well, Miss Heitschmidt, you and I will have to get together soon and discuss the music at this church. I assume you would like to continue playing?"

His graceless question didn't sit well with her, he could see. Her lowered eyebrows drew together until they looked like auburn storm clouds. "Of course. Was that in question?"

Her stern regard made him feel off-kilter. "No, um, naturally not," he spluttered, "I mean..."

"Do *you* play the organ, Reverend Williams?" she asked her voice soft in a way that warned him he was on thin ice.

"No."

"Then I had better continue, don't you think? Unless you've married an organist since we received your letter a month ago?"

Where did that sarcastic tone come from? This girl appeared as high-strung as he'd feared the church musician would be.

"Kristina," James said, laying a hand on his daughter's arm.

She spared her father a glance before returning a stern gaze to Cody's eyes that resembled the warm ocean suddenly turning to ice.

"I'm unmarried, and I'm hiding no replacement organist in my valise," he replied, unable to suppress a hint of irritation. "Your playing was lovely, and I would very much like for you to continue as you always have."

She glared another moment, letting the silence grow strained. At last, she nodded. "Thank you. I plan to do so. It was a pleasure to meet you, Reverend. Now, if you will excuse me, I have dinner to prepare. Bye, Dad." She headed for the door, lifting her shawl to cover her hair.

"Kristina, set an extra place. The reverend will be dining with us tonight."

The pale flesh between her freckles flamed, but all she said was, "Very well."

Then, scooping up a heavy black woolen coat from the last pew by the door, she bundled herself in it and left them.

Cody watched her go, puzzled about what had just happened. *I normally get along well with men and women alike. Kristina Heitschmidt must be a particularly prickly young woman.*

Shaking off the encounter, he turned his attention back to the church that would form the center of his existence for the foreseeable future. He walked up the central aisle to the altar, raising his eyes and noting the rough-hewn cross hanging behind the pulpit. Two baskets of fall flowers adorned little tables behind the rail, though they were quickly fading.

He'd passed the last several hours staring from the window of the train on his way out here and seen nothing but oceans of dry, waist-deep prairie grass crackling in the wintry wind, stretching to the horizon in all directions. Wheat fields and cattle pens only occasionally broke up the horizon. Of flowers, he had seen no sign.

I wonder how they decorate the church in the winter. Oh well, no matter. Surely there's a women's guild to tend to such matters, and its pecking order has no doubt been established long ago. He had little interest in meddling with it, provided it was more or less amicable.

Stepping behind his pulpit—which he noted was hollow in back and contained a shelf where he could place a cup of coffee—he looked out over the area that would soon be filled with his congregation.

Though he never would have admitted it, he felt a surge of apprehension as he imagined the rows of seats filled to capacity with what, from the look of the room, might well be nearly two hundred parishioners. He only knew two of them, and so far, only one had been to his liking.

Cody's eyes met those of the man who was responsible for him being here. James, the head of the elder board, had described himself in letters as a widower of middle years. He ran the general store and was designated a lay minister. *With luck, James will act as a mentor and liaison... and friend.*

It struck Cody how much James's daughter looked like him. Same features, same freckles, same hair. But on the man, it looked... ordinary, not surprising at all. To see those pugnacious attributes on a woman had given him pause.

Kristina. Thinking of the lady drew his eyes upward to the balcony. In some churches down south, such spaces contained extra seating. Here, the balcony extended across the back wall of the church, containing only the organ, which, as he had suspected, was rather too large and ornate for the town. *Still, it's a lovely instrument.*

The afternoon sun passed through the colored glass of the crucifixion scene window he'd noticed earlier, beaming in irregular patches of green and blue. They lay across the wood of the bench where, moments ago, that sharp-tongued young woman had sat, her capable, chilly fingers flying over the keys, her gray-booted feet working the pedals. Every Sunday from here until the Lord called him away, he would spend his sermon looking across the congregation and up at that woman.

I have to make peace with her, Cody decided, *even if she is a hedgehog. It's my Christian duty, and I'll do it to the best of my ability.*

Leaving the pulpit, he knelt for a moment at the altar and said a quick prayer for patience in the face of prickly and easily offended women. Then he rose, stalked to the back of the church and rejoined his host.

"Well," James asked him, "is everything in order? Will this do?"

Cody nodded. "It will do quite nicely. I'm pleased you invited me. Lord willing, this should be a good placement for me, and it's good for the congregation finally to have a full-time pastor."

James nodded. "I hope so. Kristina was right though, you know. We have a number of unmarried young women in this town, and I suspect there will soon be an unofficial 'find the new pastor a wife' competition. Are you inclined to be married?"

Cody smiled wryly. "I'm neither inclined nor opposed, I guess," he replied. "At this point, my priority is to get situated with the congregation. But I thought in Western towns, men outnumbered women, and every girl had three or four suitors to choose from."

James grinned. "You're right. There are a great many single men around here, but most are farm hands and cowboys. These girls are from middle-class families, and many of their parents would prefer them to have husbands with higher standing. It makes for a nicer life for their daughters, you know?"

"Yes, I suppose," Cody replied. His stomach rumbled. It had been a long day of travel, and his lunch had been small—just a sandwich and a cup of coffee at some stop whose name he'd forgotten five hours back along the tracks.

"Well, young man, sounds like you could use something to eat."

"Yes, please," Cody replied eagerly.

"Come on then. My house is just down the way, and I believe Kristina made beef and barley soup."

Cody's mouth watered at the thought. Pulling his coat tighter around his body, he followed James back out into the cold and stuffed his hands into his coat pockets.

James's idea of 'just down the way' meant five face-numbing blocks down Main Street.

Cody examined each house they passed to take his mind off his freezing fingers and face. Though similar in shape and size, each house differed wildly in color from its neighbors. One was sky blue with white trim, the next sage green with black, a third red with dark brown.

At last, James stopped in front of a narrow white structure. Strips of dark wood adorned the pale façade.

Cody looked up at the six steep steps that led to the covered porch and the front door. In his numb, shivering state, it looked like a mountain. His feet didn't want to lift high enough to land on the first step. Only the knowledge that up those stairs waited shelter from the biting wind forced his frozen knees to bend, bend again, and then again. At the top, he lost track of how many steps there were and stumbled on the flat surface.

The door flew open just in time to display his awkward movement to the young woman he'd met earlier. Her unpleasant expression disappeared into a look of concern. Stepping onto the icy porch, she took his arm and led him into the parlor.

For a moment, his brain felt as numb as his fingers, and he started violently as a weight urged him into a rocking chair. Something heavy landed on his lap, and something warm touched his hand.

"Dad," a female voice said in a disapproving tone, "did you bring him all that way in this flimsy coat? The poor man is half-frozen."

"It's all he had," a male voice replied defensively.

"Did you forget the charity rack in the storage room? I know there are at least three good men's coats there. They may be old and unfashionable, but they're warm, and I doubt a man of God would be worried about fashion. Especially in this cold."

It's a cup in my hand, he realized. *A cup means liquid, and it's warm.* His hand was starting to thaw, so he wrapped the other around the porcelain. It felt good. *Warm liquid can help my insides, too.* He raised it to his lips and sipped. Tea. Milk. Sugar. He sighed with pleasure.

"I forgot. Charity stuff is women's business," the male voice protested.

"Women's business, pshaw," the woman's voice sneered. "This Christmas we're reading Dickens whether you like it or not. Then we'll see whose business is what."

Cody took another deep swallow of the tea, and his brain began to focus.

13

"Dickens?" The male voice... from somewhere deep in Cody's mind, the name *James* floated up. James did not sound happy about Dickens. He was almost whining.

"Reverend Williams?" A face was in front of him. A freckled, snub-nosed face.

He blinked. "Miss... Heitschmidt?" The complicated German name barely emerged on his tongue.

"Are you all right?"

Cody downed the tea in a single scalding gulp but kept the still-warm mug clutched in his hands. At last, he felt fully awake. "Yes, thank you. I appreciate the tea... and the help."

She smiled a warm sincere smile and adjusted the weight on his lap. He glanced down to see a heavy blanket in thick, red-flecked gray wool. His eyes returned to the friendly, homely face, and he curved his lips into a smile. Only then did it occur to him how strong she must be.

Cody had passed six feet in his early teens and continued growing. He had lent his back to charity building projects and church constructions, and aided farmers, fishermen and dock-workers in their tasks. As a result, he had grown bulky and muscular, and yet this woman had steadied him with apparent ease. Now that he thought back, the top of her head had been above his shoulder, a great height for a woman. *The puppy-faced Miss Kristina Heitschmidt appears to be quite an Amazon.*

Seeing he was no longer in imminent danger of frostbite, the young woman bustled out of the room. James had also departed, leaving Cody alone in the parlor, sitting in a rocking chair beside the fireplace.

He gazed around the room. Spacious, as one would expect from one of the most influential people in town, with furniture that spoke of the Old Country. The high-backed sofa, sitting adjacent to the fireplace, was one of the most ornately carved he'd ever seen. The arms clustered with a bas-relief of vines and flowers, which echoed the scarlet roses on the black velvet upholstery.

To either side sat a black lacquer table, their tops contrasting in shades of ecru with more red flowers. On one rested an oil lamp, on the other, a fat family Bible, the leather cover etched and gilded in German. A grand piano dominated the entire room opposite the rocking chair, its lid propped half-open and sheet music spread across the stand, ready to be played at a moment's notice.

Above the sofa, a cuckoo clock with a brass pendulum had been mounted on the whitewashed wall. The swirling curlicues of open woodwork revealed gleaming gears inside.

"Reverend?" A familiar face appeared at the doorway. "Dinner is ready."

Cody rose from the rocking chair. Glancing back at it, he saw it featured carved woodwork just as fine as the clock.

He folded the blanket in half and draped it neatly over the back of the chair before following Kristina down a narrow hallway with echoing wooden floors and a prominent painting of Jesus feeding the five thousand.

She indicated an open doorway, and he entered to find a table lit with candles and set with a comforting spread of white plates and matching bowls. In the center, a silver soup tureen emitted wafts of mouth-watering beef-scented steam.

Adding to the perfume of a satisfying meal, a loaf of fresh bread sat in a basket, sliced and ready, next to a silver butter dish. A tray of cheeses had been placed on the other side of the cande-labra, as well as a platter of dried fruit.

James already sat at the head of the table, and he indicated a chair to his left.

Cody sat, unfolding an embroidered linen napkin on his lap. Kristina ladled each man a generous bowlful of soup. Cody had to tighten his lips to keep from drooling at the intoxicating aroma of beef and vegetables. He took a slice of bread, and then a pat of butter, a bit of cheese, and a small portion of prunes and dried apples.

Kristina seated herself across from him.

"Reverend Williams, would you please ask the blessing?" James requested.

Cody's stomach was cramping with hunger, so he kept his prayer brief. "Thank you, Lord, for new friends and new opportunities. I pray my work during my sojourn in this town would be blessed by you and a blessing to everyone. And Lord, I also ask your blessing on the hands that prepared this fine dinner. In your heavenly name I pray, amen."

He opened his eyes to see both Heitschmidts looking on approvingly. Then they all raised their spoons and began to eat in silence.

Kristina watched Reverend Williams eat. *Remote as Garden City is, few pastors are willing to cut themselves off from the world and minister in such a place. I hope he'll fit in here.*

It didn't seem likely. Reverend Williams was accustomed to big-city living. His application showed he'd lived in Texas all his twenty-some years of life—born and raised in Austin, attended seminary in Jacksonville, and served his first pastorate in Galveston.

With his handsome face and urban veneer, Ilse Jackson will swarm all over him. He might just be swayed by the black-haired beauty, too, if he's susceptible to flirtatious women. What a lovely matched set they would be. Their personalities should be well suited too. The young pastor seems very traditional in his thinking so far, and Ilse would appreciate that.

She could picture them together; the perfect little lady knitting, sewing, and decorating while Cody bent his head over a Bible and mapped out a fancy sermon with lots of big words and no content.

Kristina glanced around the dining room. There were no frilly feminine touches to be found in the house because she simply couldn't be bothered with them. Every piece was either a family heirloom her grandfather had brought from the old country or a gift from a friend. The house was immaculate but sparse and simple. Honestly, she preferred it that way. Fewer odds and ends meant less cleaning and therefore more time to practice on the piano in the parlor or head down to the church to visit her one true love, the pipe organ.

The clink of silver on china woke Kristina from her contemplations, and she observed Reverend Williams regarding his empty bowl and plate with a wistful expression on his face.

"Would you like some more soup?" she asked, reaching for the ladle.

"Yes, please," he replied, a white-toothed grin setting his handsome face alight.

If I were the sort to be susceptible to a good-looking man, I might have succumbed to a giggling infatuation on the spot. As it was, a sizzle shot through her belly.

She suppressed a sigh. It would be easier to embrace the spinster lifestyle if she lacked human urges. Yes, she was moved by the smile of a handsome man. Moved enough to smile back, showing her teeth. She ignored the fact that the front two were recessed, the ones on either side marginally protruding. *I'm not pretty, so what difference do misaligned teeth make? None, and I refuse to feign vanity.*

Rising, she scooped more soup into his bowl. "There's pie for dessert," she told him, "so save room."

He raised his eyebrows. "Is your pie as good as your soup?"

"Better," she admitted immodestly as she smiled again.

"I like pie. Don't worry, Miss Heitschmidt. I'll find room for both."

"After a long ride on that wretched train, I have no doubt about it."

He took another mouthful of soup, savoring the meltingly tender chunks of beef, chewing the toothsome barley, and his face took on an expression of rapture that warmed her clear to her heart. Then he swallowed and spoke. "Have you taken the train?"

"Yes. To Kansas City and home again many times. I attended a music school there several years ago."

He looked askance at her.

"Kristina, three years is not several," her father reminded her.

Now she could see the pastor mentally calculating her age.

"I'm twenty-three," she said, saving him having to ask the indelicate question. "At any rate, I know how dull the long ride across the prairie is. You came from much further. How far is it from Galveston to here?"

"Too far," he replied, and the fatigue of travel chased across his features. "But I stopped briefly in Austin to visit my parents. Who knows when I might get home again?"

"Perhaps, in time, you might come to think of Garden City as home?" Kristina suggested hesitantly.

"I'm hoping to," he replied, and then he ate another spoonful of soup, savoring it with an expression of intense concentration.

She found she quite enjoyed watching him eat. His obvious pleasure felt as good as a spoken compliment.

Cody met Kristina's eyes again. *I'm glad she got over whatever was bothering her earlier. If we can get along, it will certainly make my transition easier.* The pastor and the organist had to communicate frequently in the preparation of services, and he needed her agreeable to his leadership, not sulking.

The smiles she sent his way were growing in appeal. While no one would say she was pretty, once a person grew accustomed to her appearance, it was unfair to call her ugly. *Cute. She's cute. Like a little girl with all those freckles. There are worse things to be. I hope we can become friends.*

The rest of dinner passed in idle conversation and deep-dish apple pie with cream. He had to admit, in the far recesses of his mind, that it was better than his mother's.

Then, fed to bursting and at peace with the world, he agreed to borrow one of James's coats and a pair of gloves, a hat and a scarf, and bid his hosts goodnight.

The borrowed garments made a tremendous difference.

When he arrived at the church, joy bubbled in his soul to see smoke pouring from the chimney he could barely see behind the church. Someone had lit a fire in honor of his arrival.

I suppose was the same deacon who met the train with James and volunteered to take my suitcases to the house. Thinking hard, he remembered the young man—a banker—was named Wesley... *Fulton. That's it, Wesley Fulton.*

He traversed a walkway back behind the church. The winding path—clearly made of bricks left over from the construction of Main Street—led to a small house with a sharply peaked roof. Fumbling the key out from under his coat, Cody fitted the heavy metal rod into the lock and jiggled it, eventually making the correct contacts and opening the door.

A blast of blessed warmth spilled into the street, and Cody hurried inside wanting to keep the rest for himself. Shutting the door, he surveyed his new home. The house consisted of a single good-sized room with whitewashed tongue and groove walls and pale pine boards on the floor. In one corner, a red and tan crazy quilt covered a heavy bedstead. A low bureau acted as clothing storage and bedside table in one, and a hurricane lamp of red glass sat on top.

Opposite the bed, he noted the kitchen: a simple stove and washbasin with a hand pump set in a short stretch of wood counter below a row of three cabinets, also painted white.

To the left of the door, two high-backed armchairs flanked a loveseat with simple, green upholstery and appliquéd pillows. To the right, four wooden chairs encircled a small round table. Along the wall between the table and the bed, a bookshelf jutted from the wall.

His two suitcases waited on the table. The rest of his belongings—mostly books—would be arriving soon by freight train.

He nodded approvingly. *This is more than sufficient for my needs, and it appears comfortable and well-appointed.*

The pleasant warmth of the room quickly dispelled the cold of the night, and he removed his borrowed outerwear, tucking the hat and gloves into the pockets of the coat, which he hung on a hook mounted on the inside of the door.

He could see no sign of the necessary, but a quick peek out the back window revealed the outhouse in the yard.

He crossed to the table in three long-legged strides and opened his suitcase, removing his clothing and placing it inside the bureau.

But what to do with the suits? They'll be crushed in the drawers. He scanned the room again and noticed a curtain beside the bed. Pulling it aside, he revealed a minuscule dressing area. A clumsily constructed rack of poles with three wooden hangers dangling would suffice for storage. He placed his three suits—two brown, one black—on the hangers and closed the curtain. He set his comb, razor, brush, and mirror on top of the bureau. Last, he arranged his Bible and a few reference books on the bookshelf.

Though it wasn't particularly late, long hours of travel had left Cody weary. He hurried through the bone-chilling cold to the necessary and returned, shuddering with disgust. Some thoughtful person had left soap at the washbasin and a hand cloth hanging on a bar above, and he washed his hands, saying a brief prayer of thanks for small blessings.

Then, exhausted, Cody cleaned his teeth, stripped down to his undergarments, and slipped under the covers.

Sadly, the sheet beneath the comforter felt as icy as the night wind. It took long, shivery moments before his body heat sufficiently warmed the fabric. At last, Cody relaxed, and his eyes slid shut. His last thought before sleep bowled him under was a vision of turquoise eyes alight with laughter.

Chapter Two

Saturday morning dawned bright and crisp, the Kansas wind creeping past the cracks in the window and doorframes and chilling the little house that slumbered in the shadow of the church.

The cold rather than the light dragged Cody from his deep hibernation. A careless roll dragged the covers out of alignment, revealing one bare foot to the tickle of the icy breeze creeping under the back door. He sat bolt upright in bed. It had almost felt like a human touch on his unguarded toes. Muttering, he pulled the covers back into position as he noticed that the fire had gone out during the night, leaving the room frigid.

Cody reached over from the bed and opened the top drawer of the bureau, retrieving a pair of grey stockings before stepping into his house shoes. Covering his feet improved his mood considerably. Protected from the chilly floor, he rose and changed into clean undergarments before pulling on a pair of brown trousers, a white shirt, and his dressing gown. Quickly tying the belt of the grey and brown garment, he moved to the stove.

Cody could only cook a little—barely enough to keep body and soul together—but he could make a decent cup of coffee provided he had the right ingredients. He opened the first cabinet.

Plates, glasses, and bowls. The drawer below revealed a set of utensils.

The second cabinet was filled with staples: flour, sugar, and spices, oats and cornmeal. The drawer held a set of measuring spoons. The last cabinet renewed his faith in humanity. Coffee *and* tea for the new minister, along with cups, a kettle, and a teapot. A tin painted with tulips proved to hold some cookies.

Cody worked the pump. Frigid water flowed into the washbasin, and he caught the stream in the kettle and set it on the stove. He opened the firebox, overjoyed to see a small ember still glowing. He fed it a couple of sticks and breathed on it gently. The flame flared. Sighing with relief as warmth poured from the stove, he turned to scoop three spoonfuls of rich grounds into the coffee pot. Then he hunted out the long matches and crossed the room to the fireplace

He eyed the ashes doubtfully. He had never lit a fire in a fireplace before, as his previous homes had not been so equipped. Trying to remember what he had seen a few times in parishioners' homes, he arranged logs from a stack beside the hearth, added a few pages from the outdated newspaper left on the loveseat, and struck a match.

His first attempt proved an abject failure.

A cold draft blew down the chimney and extinguished the flame before he could even touch the paper with it. The second attempt fared little better. The third time, he managed to light the paper, but it burned to ash in seconds, not igniting the logs.

Cody realized he was going to have to ask for instruction on this process, and in the meanwhile, was going to be living in a very cold house. The kettle began to whistle, and he abandoned the fireplace so he could make his coffee.

Pouring the water over the grounds, he leaned his face down to warm it in the fragrant steam.

Returning to the first cabinet, he claimed a cup and poured himself a generous portion of liquid life, warming his hands as he held the steaming beverage under his chin. Then he took a deep sip and sighed as the warmth spread through his belly.

He carried his cup to the sitting area and settled on one of the armchairs, scooping up what remained of the newspaper and reading an article about a gang of bank and train robbers who were stirring up trouble in Southern Colorado, the panhandle of Oklahoma and Southwest Kansas. They had robbed a bank in Liberal—which Cody recalled was about forty miles away—and shot the banker, breaking his shoulder. The man had lived, but the town was in terror of a repeat attack.

Turning the page, he snorted in disgust. *The gossip section. Why do people in this small town care about the goings-on of socialites in the state capital over three hundred miles away?* Shaking his head, he turned again. Recipes and advertisements filled the last page. It appeared a small café was eking out an existence somewhere on Main Street. *That will be a welcome change from my own marginal cooking efforts now and again, provided I can afford it.*

A thundering at the door startled Cody so badly, the paper tore in his hands. It sounded as though someone was kicking the wood. He hurried to open it and gaped to see Miss Kristina Heitschmidt standing on the stoop. The reason for her using her foot to get his attention became apparent immediately. She was laden with pots—a huge one with a smaller one stacked on top. A sack hung from each arm.

"Good morning, Miss Heitschmidt," he greeted her, removing the pots from her hands. More blessed warmth radiated from them, and he carried them to the stove.

"Good morning, Reverend," she replied, setting the bags on the counter. He opened the larger pot. Soup left over from last night half-filled the large container. It brought a smile to his face. The other, smaller one made him beam. Porridge, still steaming hot and laden with plump raisins.

"You, Miss Heitschmidt, are an angel," he told her with undisguised admiration, pulling a bowl down from the cabinet and a spoon from the drawer, with which he scooped up a generous portion of the breakfast.

Her blush turned her skin darker than her freckles, but she smiled back.

"Would you like any?" he asked her.

"No, thank you. I've eaten."

"How about a cup of coffee?"

"Yes, please. It's beastly out today."

"It's not much better in here," he replied. "This is hardly a congenial environment."

"Oh, your fire went out!" she exclaimed. "Why didn't you light it?"

"I'm ashamed to admit," he told her gloomily, "I don't know how." Then he dared a glance at her face, relieved to see no mockery in her expression.

"Of course. I suppose cold is less of an issue in Texas."

"Right. And we had radiators."

"We do as well. Just not in this little house. Here, let me show you."

He set his porridge on the table and followed her to the fireplace.

"Oh, this will never work!" she explained in a gentle, neutral tone. "You have to put the fire *under* the logs."

"Why is that?" he asked.

"Because as it burns, the flames rise upwards, igniting the wood."

"That makes sense. I wonder why it didn't occur to me." He rolled his eyes toward heaven in exasperation with his lack of creativity.

Kristina gave him a tolerant grin and showed him how to construct a fire correctly. Then she set a match to the paper, which, as promised, flickered up, licking the logs until they blazed with a steady, welcoming yellow glow.

He smiled ruefully and offered her the rag to wipe her sooty hands. "How many times is it, Miss Heitschmidt, that you've saved me from the cold now? Three? You're a very considerate young woman. Thank you."

"You're welcome," she replied, scooping up her coffee.

"Are you sure it's all right for you to be here alone?" he asked. "I don't want to damage anyone's reputation, including my own."

"Yes, I'll go in a moment. I just figured you didn't have anything to eat. Along with the soup and breakfast, I also brought you some bread and cheese and some fruit."

"You should be appointed head of the welcoming committee. I suddenly feel very at home in Kansas."

"I'm glad." Her smile turned shy.

"Do you know—did your father say—whether I would be expected to prepare the service for tomorrow?"

"As a matter of fact, it's the other reason I'm here. He would like you to prepare a sermon if you would. You don't need to worry about the hymns. They've been taken care of."

He nodded. "That's reasonable."

She drained her coffee. He felt a flicker of admiration that she had drunk the strong brew black with neither cream nor sugar and hadn't reacted to its intensity in the slightest. She rinsed the cup in the washbasin and pulled a fresh cloth from the drawer, setting it on the counter with the cup inverted on top of it.

"I really must go, Reverend. The Ladies' Altar Guild is decorating the church for Christmas today, and I promised to help. They'll be expecting me."

She scooped up one of her two bags leaving the other on his counter and turned to go.

"Wait," Cody called. Kristina turned. He crossed the room and took her hand. This close, he could see she really was as tall as he remembered. At least five foot ten. He raised the hand, noting it was as heavily speckled as the rest of her, and touched his lips to her skin. "Thank you."

She gave him that friendly smile that set her eyes sparkling like the Gulf in summer before she turned and left without a word.

Cody watched from the window until she reached the end of

the brick path and turned left, heading for the door of the church. Then he sat down and savored every bite of his porridge.

Kristina lingered in his mind as he ate. *Though not pretty, she lacks neither intelligence, nor articulation, nor culinary skill. She keeps a clean house, and she possesses a ferocious talent for music. At twenty-three, someone should have married her by now. And yet she's single, like me. I wonder why.*

Though the entrance to the church was only a few steps from Reverend Williams's door, Kristina grew thoroughly chilled by the time she arrived for the church decorating party. Inside the building, a table had been set up in the entryway and piled with treats for the ladies: cookies, slices of cake, miniature tarts and urns of coffee and tea.

"Kristina!" A tall blond woman rushed over and grasped her hands, pulling her into the room.

"Good morning, Allison," Kristina replied.

"Oh good," a sarcastic voice drawled from the front, "our other Amazon is here. Ladies, the tree is out in the front. If you would be so good as to bring it inside, we have the stand ready."

Every one of Ilse's words sounded perfectly polite, but her tone left no doubt as to what she thought about these two women who didn't care as much as they should about flirting and beauty, decorations and ornaments.

Allison and Kristina grinned at each other as they headed outside. They didn't care much about Ilse either.

Sure enough, they found a huge blue spruce lying in the snow. It had come on last night's train from Colorado. The severed trunk still bled sap.

"You know, I wish I had never mentioned this tradition," Kristina commented, as she lugged the prickly evergreen up off the ground. "There are so few trees here. This one looks like it's been murdered."

"I know what you mean. I suppose in Germany they have plenty."

"I suppose. Well, maybe once it's all done up, it will look pretty."

"We can only hope," Allison concurred, and together the two women wrestled their fragrant burden through the door and up the long aisle and behind the communion rail, where a metal stand with three long screws awaited them. They carefully tipped the tree into the stand and levered it into position, making tiny adjustments while Ilse shouted advice from halfway across the room.

At last, many pricked fingers and strained muscles later, they finished the task to the satisfaction of the fussy Miss Jackson. Sighing and stretching out their Charley horses, the two women made their way back to the refreshment table. They'd more than earned a cup of tea and a snack. While they relaxed, the rest of the crew—fifteen women and seven girls ranging in age from nine to fifty—converged on the tree, affixing candles to the limbs and hanging strings of beads and little ornaments made of straw and ribbons.

While Kristina munched a juicy apple, a blast of frigid air hit her from behind. Turning, she saw Lydia Carré carrying a plate of peach turnovers, ready to join the fun.

"Lydia!" Kristina exclaimed, and Allison moved the snacks on the table to make room for the pastries. "I didn't think you'd be coming. Who's tending your café?"

"Esther," Lydia replied naming her elderly assistant. "The breakfast rush is over, and it's just soup and a sandwich for lunch today. Billy Fulton can help her serve. He's wanted to do it for a while. How's the decorating going?"

"Hard to say. I'm no expert, but it looks as though the queen of the altar guild is firmly in charge." The last Kristina said in a whisper, and Lydia squeaked with suppressed laughter.

Kristina poured a cup of coffee for Lydia and took a turnover for herself.

They watched the progress and the squabbling for several minutes before Ilse called out. "Hey, Amazons. We need one of you."

Kristina gave Allison a rueful glance and set down her half-eaten fruit, heading back up to the tree. Ilse handed her a delicate blown-glass star. It appeared to have been filled with molten gold while still soft. The shimmering metal stretched partway into each of the dozen or more little points.

Kristina stepped carefully onto a stepstool beside the spruce. Stretching out to her full height, she was just able to bend down the top of the tree and thread the bushy branch into the cone-shaped opening of the ornament. She released the stem slowly not wanting it to snap and fling the fragile star into the wall.

The entire room drew a collective breath as the tip of the tree slowly straightened. Kristina stepped down from the stool. As she had hoped, it looked cheerful and elegant in the sunlight streaming through the windows.

The group turned to the rest of the room. They affixed garlands tied with golden bows to the end of each pew and along the length of the communion rail.

Hungry after their efforts, the ladies descended on the table and devoured the snacks.

"So, Kristina, rumor has it you met the new pastor," Lydia said conspiratorially.

"Yes. He had dinner with Dad and me last night." Kristina controlled her voice, to make sure no hint of smugness emerged.

"What is he like?" Ilse asked, butting into the conversation.

"Like a pastor," Kristina replied.

"What do you mean?" the black-haired girl asked sharply, looking up at her much taller conversation partner. "Is he gray-haired and boring? Will his voice put us all to sleep?"

"Not at all," Kristina replied. "He's not a bit old. His hair is dark, and he has quite a nice voice." *He does, too. A rumbling bass I would love to add to the choir provided he can carry a tune.* Her thoughts drifted to a brief fantasy of how that would sound, and a pleasing shiver ran up her spine. *Nothing beats a bass who can truly sing.*

"Young?" Ilse's blue eyes widened.

Kristina nodded.

"But skinny? Short? He's shorter than you, isn't he? Stoop-shouldered? Does he have a limp?"

Kristina sighed knowing there would be no rest until Ilse was satisfied. "None of those things. He's tall, muscular-looking, and his hair is black, like yours. In fact, it occurred to me the two of you would match rather nicely."

Ilse snorted. "As if I would have any interest in a mere pastor when I have Carlton Holcomb courting me."

Carlton Holcomb, the son of one of the largest ranch owners in a hundred miles, had been courting Ilse for at least two years, but she refused to commit just in case someone even better came along.

"There is one thing I wanted to bring to everyone's attention, though," Kristina addressed the group, diffusing the gossip with practicality. "He's not outfitted for Kansas at all. He has a Texas coat, no gloves, no winter hat. The poor man is freezing all the time. Now I know some of you have extra garments your fathers and brothers don't need anymore. If it's for someone tall, or can be let out in the length, donate it. If you're good at knitting or crochet, put together a hat or scarf. Winter's almost here and we don't need our brand-new pastor freezing to death."

Nods of agreement around the room greeted her request.

"What about you, Kristina?" Ilse asked, in a voice just short of a sneer. "What are you going to contribute? You don't have anything, do you?"

"Actually, no. You're right. I can't knit or crochet." She forced herself to answer mildly. "I've brought him some food, and I plan to go through the charity closet and see which of the coats would be most likely to fit. It will have to suffice."

Apparently, the scripture that said a soft answer turneth away wrath was correct. Ilse could find no retort, so she remained bless-edly silent.

The discussion of the new pastor finished, the women's altar guild dispersed, heading home, some in groups, others alone, until only Kristina remained.

Though the high sun suggested lunchtime, she felt near to bursting with sweet treats and the organ was calling her. She ascended the staircase and seated herself at the bench. Her fingers tingled, but her mind raced through which pieces to practice, and in what order. A slow smile spread across her face and Kristina began to play.

Cody sat at his kitchen table, his Bible open beside him to the book of Isaiah. A concordance and two books of commentary lay nearby. He held a third. An idea bounced around in his head but refused to gel. Far too much rode on this sermon. As Saturday afternoon waned, he still had nothing to say. *Maybe nerves are getting in the way of my ability to form coherent thoughts.*

From next door, the organ began to hum. The hum rose in pitch and volume as Kristina played a series of scales, starting with the foot pedals and heading up and up across all the keyboards to piercing heights before descending.

He smiled ruefully. *Scales will do nothing but distract me.*

As though she'd heard the thought, the crawling notes ended, and a slow, melancholy tune played in a minor key emerged from the church next door.

"'Rejoice, rejoice,'" Cody sang, "'Em-man-uel shall come to thee oh Israel.'" *Anticipation, excitement, apprehension. Waiting for someone to arrive. Waiting to arrive. Not knowing what might happen. It's like waiting for Christmas. We wait with joy because we know the end of the story, but the children of Israel didn't know. They had prophecies but didn't understand them. It's like a pastor coming to a new church. Like a church receiving a new pastor...*

Like a match flaring to life, the entire sermon burst into Cody's head. He knew just what he needed to say.

Trusting the idea would not leave in a moment, he offered a quick prayer of thanks before reaching for his pencil and beginning to scribble furiously on his paper.

Chapter Three

Sunday morning found Cody standing behind the pulpit of his new church, waiting for the organist to arrive. She came early, of course, so she could begin the prelude before the congregation started to file in.

"Miss Heitschmidt," he called to her, and she jumped. "Sorry, I didn't mean to startle you. I have a request. I know you said the music would already be taken care of for today, but I would like the sermon hymn to be 'O Come, O Come, Emmanuel'."

She looked at him from across the room but said nothing.

"Is that a problem?" he asked.

"I suppose not. I was saving it for advent next week, but..."

"You still can. Do it both times. It ties in with my sermon."

"I don't usually use the same hymn two weeks in a row." The cold tone had returned to her voice.

Irritated, he said sharply, "It makes no difference to me whether you play it next week or not, but I want it for the sermon hymn today."

"You're the pastor," she said with a sigh.

Instead of climbing the stairs to the balcony, she walked up the aisle and opened a door to the far-left side of the communion rail. A moment later, she emerged with a battered wooden box.

Quickly snagging a hymnal from the back of the nearest pew, she leafed through the green book and set it open on the seat. From a board set with pegs that hung on the wall near the front, she removed three thin plaques with numbers on them and replaced them with new ones. Setting the old numbers in the box, she crossed the front of the sanctuary to the other side and repeated the process with an identical board on that side.

"Is that where the hymns of the day are posted?" he asked

"Yes," she snapped, her voice clipped. Anger seemed to radiate off her.

"Do you normally set them?"

"Of course. I'm the organist." Her sharp tone made him feel like an imbecile.

"Well, don't you think it's a good idea for me to know how it works? In case you were ill or out of town or something?" Cody tried to suppress his irritation at her unexpected prickliness by reciting the fruits of the spirit in his mind. *Love, joy, peace...*

"I suppose. The numbers are in the box. They hang on the pegs. The box is on the shelf in the storage room, next to the crowns."

"Crowns?"

"For Christmas plays," she drawled, as though any child would know that's what they were for.

Patience, kindness, goodness... "Of course. Thank you, Miss Heitschmidt."

"Is there anything else, or may I go and practice now?"

"No, that's it."

She stomped up the stairs hard enough to make the wood rattle.

Faithfulness, gentleness, self-control. Oh Lord, grant me self-control with this woman. She switches from pleasant to surly without warning.

The organ began to hum, and a moment later, Kristina crashed out a loud and dissonant chord. It startled him so much he banged his knee on the pulpit.

He scowled at her, but of course, she had her back to him and couldn't see. He knew she had heard the reverberation of flesh against hollow wood though. He could imagine her smirk.

Shaking his head and rubbing his developing bruise, he checked for the hundredth time to be sure his notes were in order. Then, glancing at his pocket watch, he pulled on his borrowed coat and headed to the door to greet the arrivals.

James Heitschmidt ambled up the street and mounted the stairs. He shook Cody's hand and greeted him warmly.

Next came a family with three daughters who appeared to be in their early twenties: pretty blonds with warm brown eyes and rather vacant expressions. They wore matching blue wool pea coats and matching insipid smiles.

I wonder how I'll ever tell them apart. They look like they were rolled out on a printing press. Their mother, a shrewd, dark-eyed woman, introduced them as April, May, and June. He tried not to roll his eyes, especially when he learned their last name was Day.

Another family approached, then another. Next, a dark-haired man with a pencil-thin mustache escorted an attractive woman through the door. A teenage boy and a young woman with striking blue eyes in a lovely face trailed after him. A wisp of black hair slipped out from under the young woman's white knitted hat.

"Paul Jackson." The man shook Cody's hand with a bit more pressure than was necessary. It didn't hurt Cody's calloused palm, but he felt sure it was intended as a mild intimidation tactic. "My wife, Gretchen, and our daughter Ilse. This is our son, Frederick."

Cody nodded to each in turn.

Gretchen gave him a snooty look, pursing her lips as she looked him up and down. Ilse, however, gazed at him with frank admiration and a flirtatious little tilt of her head.

He felt nothing, despite her beauty.

Shrugging off his unexpected lack of reaction, he greeted the next people in line: an elderly couple, and then a young family with a swarm of red-haired boys milling around the feet of their parents. The children's threadbare clothes made it obvious their father struggled to provide for such a brood. "Charles Wade," the man introduced himself. "Sheriff's deputy. This is my wife, Miranda." She smiled distractedly, and they herded the unruly pack into the church and began arranging them in a pew, trying to keep all the boys separated.

On and on it went, until Cody's head swam. At last, his pocket watch showed 10:30 and he shut the heavy door. The organ, which had been playing prelude music for the last hour, completed one last verse while he made his way back to the pulpit.

"Good morning," he began, and the crowd returned the greeting in a rumbling murmur. "I'm so glad to be here with you today. In case you haven't heard, my name is Cody Williams, and I've been called to be pastor of this congregation. I look forward to getting to know all of you, which I promise to do... eventually." A wave of chuckles ran through the room. "During the sermon, I'll tell you all a little more about myself, but for now, let's get started with our opening hymn."

As he had hoped, the congregation had already found the correct page. From the balcony, he could see Kristina's back as she began to crash out the chords. Then he noticed she wasn't alone. He'd been mistaken in assuming the balcony contained no seating. A double row of adults, men in back, women in front, sat beside the organ. *How interesting. No one mentioned a choir.*

Cody returned his attention to the service, which progressed quite normally. Songs, scriptures and announcements all passed by in their customary sequence. Next on the agenda, according to his notes, would be the offering.

While a group of ushers passed the plates down the aisles, Cody noticed movement on the balcony. Kristina had risen from her organ bench and stood in front of the choir. She made a sweeping gesture and the group rose as one. Then she lifted her arms, beating out a quick tempo with a swinging movement of her hands. Cody had taken two requisite music courses at the seminary, but he'd never mastered such a fluid conducting stroke.

Four beats in, the ladies opened their mouths, inhaled silently, and began. "'Come thou Lo-ng Expected Je-sus'."

They sang in unison, the warbly-voiced older women doing their best to blend with the younger ones, so it almost sounded like a single voice. In the second phrase, they split into two-part harmony for "'From our fears and sins release us'." Two lines later, the tenors joined in on "Israel's strength and consolation," and for the last two, the basses added a low-pitched, rumbling foundation on "'Dear desire of every nation.'"

Cody found himself nodding. *For a simple hymn arrangement, it's quite effective and attractively presented.*

The second verse began with all parts in harmony on "'Born thy people to deliver,'" but when they commenced the next phrase, Cody noticed they sang without a director. Kristina had slipped back to the organ adding a rolling accompaniment line with one hand, and then both, and at last, at the end of the second verse, she added foot pedals, so an intricate blending of vocal and instrumental music reverberated through the cavernous interior of the church.

The song ended. The ushers brought the offering plates to the front where Cody prayed over them, fumbling his words as the music echoed in his brain. Then he pulled himself together as James gathered the plates and he and Wesley walked around to the side opposite the storage room, where Cody had earlier noticed a small office. The congregation, as requested, opened their hymnals and sang "'O Come, O Come Emmanuel.'"

As the hymn ended, Cody knelt at the altar, closed his eyes and prayed under his breath, "Lord, make my words meaningful to the people in front of me. Help me strengthen their faith." Then he rose and approached the pulpit.

"Good morning, again. I'm so thankful to y'all for bringing me here," he said, watching them smile at his soft, Texas drawl. "I hope, Lord willing, we all learn to pull together, to make this a real community of faith in action. That's one thing you'll learn about me. I'm not a pastor who stands in the pulpit making speeches and then goes home. I'll be out among you, giving my all, helping in whatever way I can and generally making a nuisance of myself."

Polite chuckles.

"For our service this morning, I asked our esteemed music leader if she would kindly change her plan for the hymn so we could have that beloved Advent song fresh on our minds. I chose it because of how it talks about waiting for some joyous event. If you would, please turn in your Bibles to the book of Isaiah."

Paper rustled amongst the congregation. Cody gave them a moment to settle. Leafing through the Old Testament could be tricky, but at last, the majority of the paper crackling stilled, and faces looked up to see what he was going to say next.

"So, as I'm sure you know, Isaiah was a prophet from the past. He lived long before Jesus's birth, but he predicted the coming Messiah. It was kind of like... getting a letter saying a new pastor is coming. You know it's going to happen. You even know some details about it, but until the time comes, you don't really understand what it's going to be like."

He paused, giving them time to digest his words. "Imagine, if you will, the Children of Israel. They knew a Messiah was coming to save them, but they had no idea what it meant. From our perspective, having read the whole story, it seems obvious—but to them? What did they think about it all? Try to imagine knowing nothing about Christ but what you read in this passage. Wouldn't you be puzzled by the phrase, 'the Lord has laid on him the iniquity of us all'? Or 'by his stripes, we are healed'? They had no idea it would be meant literally."

He turned over his page of notes. "Now, for me, being the pastor who was coming, I also didn't know what to expect. I knew some facts: the size of the town, its location, the names of a few people, but I had no idea how cold and windy it would be here, and I wasn't prepared. There's still a lot I don't know about this town, and about y'all. But I'm ready and willing to learn, to find my place here. To help and lead."

He paused for the length of a long breath. "Now, friends, think about this. Christ knew *exactly* what he was facing when he came. He knew how this story would end. He knew he would bear our griefs and carry our sorrows. He knew he would be wounded for our transgressions and bruised for our iniquities. He came anyway. That is a love beyond our ability to comprehend, and I thank God for it. Let's pray."

The congregation, stunned into silence by the hard-hitting point, bowed their heads obediently. Cody prayed a long time, but only the smallest children began to squirm. When he finished, they sang one last hymn and the service concluded.

As he stood again at the back of the church, shaking people's hands and wishing them a good afternoon, he reflected on how well it had gone... better than he'd expected. He couldn't take credit for it. Sometimes the Lord just took him over. He found it disconcerting when it happened—but exciting too.

"Well, Reverend, would you like to come to lunch with us today?"

Cody looked up, discovering James had invited him.

"Oh, Mr. Heitschmidt," a sultry voice behind him cooed, "you can't keep him all to yourself. We'd like to have him to lunch at our place today. What do you say, Reverend? Will you come eat with us?"

His gaze turned to the pretty, black-haired girl who had flirted with him earlier. *Elsie, was it? No, Elise... that doesn't sound right either. This is going to take a while.*

She seemed to sense his trouble. "Ilse Jackson."

A glance at Mrs. Jackson showed her looking over the other women of the congregation with a condescending smirk. *Why would such a snooty family want me for lunch anyway?*

Cody suppressed a sigh. *There's a family like this in every congregation. Might as well get it over with.*

"Miss Jackson. Yes, I would be delighted to accept your invitation. Thank you. James, some other time, okay? I need to meet everyone."

James nodded. "Don't forget you're meeting with the elder board this afternoon."

"I won't forget." *Of course I won't. They'll be discussing my salary.*

Ilse's lips curved into a sultry smile, and she batted her eyelashes.

He gave her a friendly but impersonal grin and turned to the next person. Turquoise eyes bored into his with intensity and a hint of uncertainty.

"Miss Heitschmidt, I appreciate you changing the hymn for me. I imagine it's difficult to do at the last second, so thank you."

She seemed mollified by his thanks. "You're welcome. Maybe in the future, we can meet ahead of time and plan it out so there's less confusion."

Ah, good. A perfect lead-in. "Yes, ma'am, we do need to meet. Is there a time tomorrow we could get together?"

"Certainly. Would you like to meet for lunch at Lydia's?"

"If I can find it," he said, with a self-deprecating grin.

"It's just up the street." She indicated a two-story white structure with a sign over the door, the name of the proprietress painted in bold black cursive. The wooden shingle clunked in its metal frame as the wind sent it flapping.

"Oh," Cody said, his grin widening when he realized how near the place was. "I think I can manage. How's the food?"

"It's great," she explained. "If you go to the hotel, you might never get anything to eat. They're very slow. Lydia has a limited menu, but everything on it is delicious and reasonably priced."

"Then I think meeting there tomorrow for lunch would be perfect. Until then, Miss Heitschmidt." He ended the handshake with a gentle squeeze.

She gave him one of her appealing, freckle-faced smiles and moved on, letting the trapped parishioners out from behind her before the grumbling could commence in earnest.

As the last elderly couple made their unsteady way down the

steep stairs, Cody met the eyes of his lunchtime hosts, who waited in the biting cold to escort him to their home.

He ducked inside to retrieve his borrowed winter wear. Shoving his hands into the gloves, he followed his hosts down the street. A frigid wind whistled between the buildings and nipped him squarely on the end of his nose. The cold took his breath away. *It isn't even December yet, and I'm already freezing.*

"Is it always this windy in Kansas?" he wheezed.

"Usually," Paul shouted over his shoulder. "The wind always blows. The only thing that changes is the temperature."

"That's good to know."

Unlike the Heitschmidts, the Jacksons only lived a block and a half away from the church. They turned left at the corner, passing a wind-blasted oak tree with no leaves and a couple of small square boxes of homes before arriving at a two-story in dusty blue with black trim and ostentatious shutters on each window.

Paul ushered Cody into a sitting room of suffocating coziness. Hand-embroidered pillows in shades of blue and black piled high on each of the sofas. The legs of both shone with black lacquer, as did the stiff, high-backed chairs, end tables, and the fireplace mantle. The floors, pale pine, added almost no color to the room. It took Cody a minute to realize it matched the women's coloring. *Black hair. Blue eyes. It makes sense in a vain sort of way.*

"Have a seat," Mrs. Jackson urged. "Lunch won't be ready for a little while."

Cody eyed the sofa, but Ilse sank gracefully onto it, so he chose one of the hard, black armchairs. The seat lacked comfort, but it kept the little flirt from scooting closer and closer to him. She had a predatory expression, and it made him uncomfortable.

"So, Reverend," Paul said, sitting on the sofa adjacent to his daughter, "what do you think of our little town so far?"

"It's windy," he replied, and the Jacksons laughed. "I'm sure, once I get to know everyone, it will be fine. It might take a while though. It's a pretty big congregation."

"One hundred eighty-six souls, and two more due to arrive in the spring," Paul told him proudly.

"That's a lot of names to learn."

"Ilse, why don't you go get your photograph?" Paul suggested. "Lend it to Reverend Williams and give him a list of everyone's names so he can study them."

Ilse's eyes flashed with excitement, and she scampered out of the parlor.

Cody wanted to sigh. He didn't do it, but he wanted to. Looking at a photograph together meant sitting shoulder to shoulder. *I wonder if her father is trying to push us together. It seems unlikely, as I'm hardly a catch. Pastor is far from a glamorous job, and I don't even have enough money at the moment to buy myself a new hat.*

Knowing he would have to do this, he moved to the sofa in anticipation of Ilse's return. Moments later she hustled back into the room with a piece of paper, a pencil, and a photo displayed in a black lacquer frame.

She settled down next to him, and as he had feared, her shoulder pressed firmly against his arm. She set the photo on his lap and peered at it, and Cody bent his head to study it.

The faces he had seen this morning looked up at him, devoid of color and smiles but still recognizable. He identified the Jacksons. Ilse, an adolescent in this picture, was still too beautiful to be real. Their son Frederick was a chubby-cheeked boy. Near them stood James Heitschmidt, a lovely woman at his side, a young man standing behind him. Of his daughter, there was no sign.

"Where's Miss Heitschmidt?" Cody asked.

Ilse scowled at the mention of the other woman. "This photo was taken three years ago," she said as though that answered the question.

It told Cody nothing. "Where was she?" he insisted.

Ilse sighed in irritation. "She was away at music school. She was there for three years. One more year and she would have completed her course of studies."

"Ah, yes. She mentioned that at dinner. Why didn't she finish?"

Ilse indicated the photograph. "This is Kristina's mother, Gertrude. She got cholera and died about two months after this photograph was taken."

"Cholera?" Cody met his host's gaze, concerned.

Paul crimped his lips. "There was a bad outbreak right about the time Ilse said. We lost the pastor, his wife, Elder Heitschmidt's wife and about half the rest of the town. It's when we decided to construct the city sewer. Safer water, you know? Nearly all the houses opted to connect, and we haven't had another case since."

"Good to know the town takes these things seriously." He bent over the picture again. "Who's this?"

"Kristina's brother, Calvin," Ilse explained, sounding sulky.

"I didn't know she had a brother. Where is he?"

"He went off to seek his fortune. He hasn't been seen or heard from since."

"And Kris... "He cleared his throat. "That is to say, Miss Heitschmidt came home..."

Ilse glanced sharply at his slip of accidentally using a near stranger's first name, but she answered, nonetheless. "Just before her mother died. She could have gone back, maybe, but then her brother left. She couldn't stand for her father to be alone. That, and Mr. Heitschmidt couldn't afford the tuition anymore. So here she is."

"What a shame."

"It is for her," Ilse sneered. "She needed a career. It's not like she'll ever find a husband looking the way she does."

"Miss Jackson!" Cody exclaimed. "How rude. That's no way for a Christian woman to be talking. As though a woman's looks are the only things to recommend her. Might I remind you, looks fade? Miss Heitschmidt is a kind and talented woman, and to some men, that might be more appealing than a pretty face."

Cody colored. He'd revealed things he hadn't fully realized himself. *Could it be true? Could I be drawn to Miss Heitschmidt?* He shook off the image of her freckled face and realized the Jacksons were staring at him.

Recovering, Paul spoke to his daughter sternly. "Ilse, you apologize. It isn't right to speak of Miss Heitschmidt so harshly. She can't help the way she looks."

"I'm sorry," Ilse choked, her face flaming. Then she rose stiffly to her feet and fled the room.

Cody knew he'd gone a bit far, but Ilse's unwarranted attack needed to be addressed. *I will not let snobbery go unchallenged in my congregation, and they will either acquiesce or throw me out.*

Poor Miss Heitschmidt. Missing out on her studies so close to completion, losing her mother and her brother in the space of a few months, and being trapped in this tiny town. No doubt being bullied by that little brat. No wonder her moods vacillate so wildly.

Lunch turned out to be a strained and silent affair, the food showy but tasteless. Ilse refused to come down from her room. After overcooked roast beef with bland potatoes and mushy vegetables, followed by apple pie that tasted of sugar and little else, Cody glanced at his pocket watch. "Thank you for your hospitality, but I must go. The elder board is meeting shortly, and I need to be there."

He shook Paul's hand, pretended not to notice Gretchen's sour look, and bundled himself up to walk back to the church.

The elders—James Heitschmidt, John Fulton, William Schultz and Louis Claiborne—sat around the small table in the office behind the sanctuary. Cody looked over the four men who were responsible for him being here and wondered if they would approve or disapprove of his actions today. Not that he regretted anything, but it was, perhaps, not the best introduction to the town.

Pushing aside his embarrassment, he focused his attention on the meeting.

Chapter Four

Monday at noon, Cody made his way slowly down the street. The wind blew as strongly as ever, but today the sun had managed to come out, raising the temperature into the lower 50s. Even for his thin Texas blood, this felt tolerable. Glad to don his own coat, he buttoned the brown wool up to his chin.

As he walked along, his mind returned to the strange feelings he'd had the previous day. *I defended Miss Heitschmidt. I told Miss Jackson there was more to a woman than her face. and I meant it. There's something about Kristina Heitschmidt I want to get to know better. If only I could figure out what it is I do that sometimes upsets her, I'm sure I'll be able to tease her out of it.*

Deciding to start with lunch, he pulled open the door of the café, he stepped across the threshold. The restaurant inside was cheerful, if shabby. The floorboards curled up in several spots. Flour sack curtains shaded the windows but had been pinned back to admit as much of the welcome sunshine as possible. Twelve round tables sat at regular intervals around the room, covered in red checkerboard tablecloths.

A plump woman with round pink cheeks, wearing a gingham dress with the sleeves pushed up to the elbows, served meals on white plates. Another woman—older with thin grey hair pulled up into a wispy bun—rang up sales behind a mahogany countertop.

Scanning the room, Cody quickly located Kristina's freckled, snub-nosed face. She sat in the corner near the window, letting the sunlight warm her. He joined her quickly, seating himself across from her so he could look into her pretty, turquoise eyes.

She greeted him with a smile, but it was a wary smile, not relaxed like before. She seemed... nervous.

He didn't like it.

"Miss Heitschmidt," he said. "I'm so glad to see you."

"Reverend." That was all she said. Just his title. It bothered him.

He was about to speak when the proprietress breezed up, a plate in each hand, each laden with a strange-looking pillow of bread. The aroma rising from the steaming rolls smelled of many wonderful things besides yeast and flour. She set them on the table before the couple, winked at Kristina, and bustled away.

"What's this?" he asked.

"A bierock," she replied.

He quirked an eyebrow. "Beer rock?"

"No." Kristina couldn't suppress a grin. "There's no beer in them. Just cabbage, minced beef, and onion."

"Sounds tasty."

"It is."

Cody picked up a hot bun and took a bite. He beamed at Kristina. "This is wonderful."

Instead of responding, she broke eye contact with him.

Stung by the rebuke, Cody reached across the table and clasped her hand. "Was it really so terrible that I asked you to change one hymn?"

"Of course not." Color bloomed on her speckled cheeks. "You're the pastor. It's your right to choose hymns to align with your sermon. I'm sorry for being so touchy. I'm afraid I'm a little... territorial about the music." She took a bite of her lunch, using only her free hand and letting him keep his hold on the other.

"Understandable. You're quite a musician."

Her blush took on a different quality this time, and she smiled for real, her eyes sparkling. He smiled back.

Is she homely? Did I think so? I don't see it anymore. She's well worth looking at. "Have you really been doing all the music for the church for the last three years?"

"Yes," she replied.

"Well, you can finally relax, darlin'." Though not a man prone to using casual endearments, this one felt right. "I've studied music a little. You will not need to do that anymore. I will take over the choir, choosing hymns, all of it. You only need to play the organ."

Kristina looked far from overjoyed at this information. "It's no trouble."

"I insist. You have been asked to do more than your share for three years. Won't it feel good to tend to women's business again?"

Her eyes narrowed, the color turning icy. "Women's business?" she asked, her voice even colder than her expression.

What did I say now? His eyebrows drew together in consternation. "Yes."

"And just what do you think that would be?"

"Cooking, caring for your home, helping your dad. Finding a suitor..." he gave her a look that he hoped said more than his words revealed.

"I don't want a suitor, and I have plenty of time to take care of all my 'women's business'. It's not a hardship for me to direct the choir." If she'd sounded cold the other day, today icicles dripped from her tone.

"It's not appropriate for a woman to teach or lead men."

Her eyes narrowed to disapproving slits. "I see." She pulled her hand out of his, pushed her chair back, and stalked to the counter, setting a coin on the wood.

Then she fled out the door before he could even process what had happened.

Kristina barely made it outside before the burning tears in her eyes spilled down her cheeks. Cursing daintily under her breath, she scrubbed at her face but failed to stem the flow.

She began to run, her only thought to get home before she broke down completely.

She didn't even come close to succeeding.

Chapter Five

After that day, Cody had to endure nothing but coldness from Kristina. His hopes had been utterly dashed. She barely spoke to him while they prepared for Sunday's service. He told her what hymns he wanted, and she played them, but her performance had become erratic. Sometimes she blasted the congregation with unwarranted passion. Other times she played listlessly with little attention to the rhythm, hitting the wrong notes.

The following Wednesday night, after his abysmal failure of a first attempt at directing the choir, he sat in front of his fireplace, sipping tea morosely.

"What is wrong with them? Why did they sing so well when I first came and so badly now? Why were they so unwilling to follow the simplest directions? I know they're used to a certain sort of direction, but honestly, if I have to listen to 'Miss Heitschmidt does it this way', or 'Kristina doesn't do it like that' one more time, I think I'm going to lose my mind."

He set his cup on the table and flung himself backwards against the upholstery. "They'll just have to get used to it. I'm in charge here now. Of course, there will be adjustments, but they'll eventually learn to work with me."

Despite his determination, he couldn't help but feel something more was lacking than just a certain unfamiliarity with his style.

❀

Two weeks later, the stalemate continued. So did the tension in the choir. As he fumbled with the Christmas cantata music, which was, in his opinion, too hard for a church choir—particularly one that refused to accept instruction—his frustration grew.

Now he knelt again at the altar, praying for various members of the congregation while struggling with his wandering mind. "Lord, please heal Mrs. Fulton of her lung congestion and a bad cough."

His attention strayed.

Sundays are going swimmingly. The congregation enjoys my sermons, and the other parts of the service mesh as well. I'm only struggling with the music, as always. While he enjoyed singing, he did not feel confident about directing, but a town this small had no need of a music minister, and the church couldn't afford one.

In an effort to keep their new pastor happy, they'd decided to pay him quite a generous salary. He had more than enough to buy himself winter wear, but none had been needed.

One week after his arrival, a welcome basket had appeared on his doorstep during the night. Inside, he had found a black woolen coat with twice the warmth of the thin one he'd brought, along with a knitted hat, scarf, and mittens, all practically vibrating in a vivid shade of blue. He could see immediately which family had organized the offering.

Now he felt well equipped for the Kansas weather, and not a moment too soon because winter was bearing down on them with frightening speed. Every morning, frost swirled on his windowpanes. Only last night, fat flakes of snow had begun drifting from the sky as he walked the short brick path from the church to the vicarage. He knew little about snow, and he'd

49

enjoyed watching it until a snowflake had landed on the end of his nose. The cold wetness had burned him, and after that, he'd been glad to hurry inside where a cheerful fire awaited.

"Prayers, Pastor," he reminded himself. "You're twitchy as a seven-year-old boy. Focus. Lord, also please bring healing to Ilse Jackson's brother, who fell in the street and broke his arm. And what on earth am I going to do about Ilse herself?"

Lord, I don't think this girl really likes me, and I certainly don't care for her, he added internally, formal prayers giving way to an earnest plea. *Can you please encourage her to stop flirting with me? It looks bad and leads nowhere. I have no interest in Ilse Jackson. Find her a husband, Lord, so she stops bothering me. And please, Lord, help me figure out what to do with this choir. I can't understand what I'm doing wrong, and I want it to be...*

What Cody wanted it to be, he never got the chance to express. At that moment the door burst open, and Allison Spencer flew into the church, her coat misbuttoned.

"Pastor, you have to come right away. Please hurry!" she panted.

"What's going on?" he asked, bewildered. Miss Spencer, he had learned in recent weeks, was a good friend of Kristina's. She worked at the mercantile with Kristina's father. The tall blond was a pleasant, forthright woman, a spinster in her mid-twenties with no prospects but happy enough in spite of it.

She did not look happy now—in fact, she looked frantic. She was wringing her hands and gnawing on her lip. A thin trickle of blood ran down her chin. She didn't seem to notice.

"What's wrong?" Cody asked again, alarmed by the woman's panic.

"It's Wesley's wife," she blurted, her hand on her chest as she struggled to force words past a tongue that seemed unwilling to cooperate.

"Calm down, Miss Spencer. What happened to Wesley's wife?"

"She fell through the ice on the river. They just brought her home."

"Is she ill?" *Stupid question, Williams, of course she's ill! She just took a plunge into icy water!*

"She's dead! Oh, heavens, Reverend, you have to come. Wesley is alone with her body. I didn't want to leave him, but he needs help."

Cody flew into his coat and was out the door in less than ten seconds.

While he'd been inside praying, the sky had darkened, growing cloudy and ominous. A chilly drizzle began falling, coating the sidewalk in nearly invisible ice. Cody struggled to keep his footing on the slick surface. Allison lost hers once, her smooth-soled boots going out from under her and leaving her sprawled on a dry, brown lawn. Cody hauled her to her feet with less gentility than he would normally have afforded.

The Fulton home lay two blocks down the street. In his hurry, Cody hardly noticed the wide, warped porch, the peeling yellow paint, the crooked shutters the color of trees in summer.

He and Allison ran to the front door and entered without knocking. As Allison grasped his elbow and pulled him through the house, he got a brief flash of a spacious but poorly maintained parlor, a kitchen with a filthy counter, and at last, a scuffed, wooden staircase, which they ascended far more quickly than was wise.

She led him along the upstairs hallway to a closed door. From behind low, choking sobs emanated.

Allison reached for the knob, but her trembling hand failed to grasp it firmly. Cody took over.

In the yellow-painted room, a woman's voluptuous figure, clad in a wet gray dress, lay on a sagging bed covered with a stained and torn white blanket. Her face had been covered with a handkerchief. It did not move.

On a chair beside the bed, a handsome young man with

mahogany brown hair clutched a little girl to his chest and sobbed.

"Wesley?" Cody laid one hand on the man's shoulder.

Wesley turned towards him, his eyes red and swollen. His breath rasped and wheezed as he struggled to inhale. Allison approached, laying her hand on Wesley's arm. He grasped her fingers in a crushing grip. Allison winced but didn't protest.

"Wesley, I..." Cody had no words, no ideas. His mind had gone blank. He looked at Wesley and Wesley looked back. He seemed as though he were the one drowning, and Cody had not a clue what to do for him.

Lord, help Wesley. Do something for him, I can't even think of one word. Help me to help him.

Wesley stood and thrust his little girl into Cody's arms. Then he embraced Allison, squeezing her hard and receiving her crushing hug.

Cody turned his attention to the child in his arms. She regarded him solemnly. With her long blond braids, she didn't much resemble her father except perhaps those dark eyes.

Cody liked children well enough, of course, but nothing in his training had prepared him to hold a toddler two feet away from her mother's corpse while her father wept.

"Are you the pastor?" she asked, her words barely understandable under a series of babyish lisps.

"Yes."

"Can we pray, pastor?"

"Of course."

"I wanna start. God, please make my daddy not be sad. Please help my mommy go home."

Cody's throat burned. Three adults in the room and only the three-year-old knew what to say.

A clatter of boots sounded on the wooden boards of the stairs, and then the hallway, and more people hurried into the room. One was Kristina, the other a short, plump woman Cody recognized as Wesley's mother.

"Son?"

Wesley raised his head from Allison's shoulder.

"Mama. She's..." Wesley's voice broke.

The older woman crossed quickly to her son and shoved Allison away, embracing him herself.

Allison stumbled, and Kristina caught her arm, steadying her.

"Auntie Allie?" the child said.

"Yes, Missy?" In response, the little girl held out her arms and Allison plucked her away from Cody. "Come on, honey. Let's get out of here."

"I want to give Papa another hug."

Allison brought Wesley his daughter, and she kissed him on the cheek. "I love you," she told him. Allison carried her out of the room.

"Mrs. Fulton," Kristina said hesitantly, "Wesley shouldn't be in here either."

"I..." he stopped, cleared his throat, and tried again. "I can't leave her."

"Wesley, she's gone," Cody told him gently, "and we have to try to think a bit."

Among the three of them, they managed to drag Wesley away from his wife's body and down the stairs to the disheveled parlor.

"I'll make us some tea," Kristina offered, sweeping from the room.

Wesley's mother urged him down on the threadbare sofa facing the fire. She sat next to him and patted his hand.

"This is my fault," Wesley said at last.

"No," his mother protested. "It was an accident. She went through the ice."

"Why was she out on the ice? Everyone knows it's not safe. The river never freezes hard enough to stand on. It must have been intentional."

"Wesley," Cody crouched in front of his friend, meeting his eyes, "that doesn't make it your fault."

"I knew she was... unstable. She's... tried things before. I shouldn't have left her. It's enough I work all day. There's no way I should be doing these other things; going to church, being a deacon. She never liked it."

"You could have brought her with you," Cody reminded him.

"She wouldn't go. Called them a bunch of two-faced hypocrites. There was... gossip, about her, at the church. They weren't nice to her there." Wesley fell silent again.

"I'm sorry to hear it," Cody told him. "I would never have permitted it. I promise you, Wesley, she's going to have a beautiful funeral, right there at the church, and I don't care what anyone says about it."

A rattling noise diverted attention to the doorway, where Kristina stood holding a tray of cups and tea accessories in shaking hands.

Mrs. Fulton jumped from the sofa and rescued the tea service before Kristina could drop it.

Wesley looked at the teapot, bewildered, as though wondering where it had come from. He seemed to be going into shock.

Cody stood and retrieved a ragged lap blanket from the back of a scarred rocking chair. Bringing it to Wesley, he wrapped it around the man's trembling shoulders.

Mrs. Fulton poured tea into a delicate rose-patterned teacup with a gilded handle, sugared it heavily, and handed it to her son. The tiny cup looked ludicrous in his calloused hand, and Cody had to fight down a shout of wildly inappropriate laughter.

"Pastor, I..." Wesley was looking at Cody with those wild haunted eyes again. "What am I going to do? How can I take care of Melissa alone?"

"Wesley, I'm going to be real honest. I'm not sure how exactly you're going to make your life work now. Things will change, that's for certain. But you'll never be alone." He squeezed the man's arm, promising a physical presence as well as a divine one.

Wesley handed the untouched tea back to his mother and buried his face in his hands.

"Let's pray," Cody suggested, finding his voice at last. "Lord

God, we cry out to you today for your comfort for Wesley. Help him, Lord. Remind him he's not alone. He has friends and family who love him, and you will never leave him." Cody ran out of words again, but an inaudible whisper gave him a scripture to use. "'The Lord is my shepherd. I shall not want.'"

"'He maketh me lie down in green pastures.'" Kristina joined him. "'He leadeth me beside the still waters. He restoreth my soul.'"

A third voice chimed in. Allison, still holding Melissa, entered the room and sat down beside Wesley. "'He leadeth me down the paths of righteousness for his name's sake.'"

Wesley spoke too, his voice breaking on the next line. "'Yea, thou I walk through the valley of the shadow of death, I shall fear no evil, for thou art with me. Thy rod and thy staff, they comfort me. Thou preparest a table before me in the presence of mine enemies. Thou annointest my head with oil; my cup runneth over. Surely goodness and mercy shall follow me all the days of my life, and I will dwell in the house of the Lord forever.'"

"Amen," Cody added. "That's where she is now, Wesley. In the house of the Lord. There's no better, safer place for her than there."

Wesley nodded. As comforts went, it was almost worse than useless. The grief was too fresh for platitudes, however true they might be.

Allison hugged Wesley again, and he turned in her embrace, enfolding Melissa between them.

Wesley had found his comfort, so Cody took Kristina's elbow, leading her to the corner of the room. He indicated the rocker beside the stove and perched in the brass-studded blue armchair opposite it. In the trauma of their friend's loss, they dropped animosity between them with a single, intense look.

"Do you think Wesley will want any say in planning the funeral?" he asked her.

"I don't know. He doesn't look up to it."

"Why didn't the people of the church like his wife?"

"She was a bit... wild. There was gossip because she was already expecting when they married. Some even say Melissa isn't his daughter."

"Ouch," Cody winced.

"There was opposition to him becoming a deacon because of it, but he's well-liked and good at counting money, so he was accepted in the end."

"Well, all that's in the past. The least we can do is give her a wonderful funeral. Show people we're not throwing stones. I won't have this kind of behavior anymore."

"I'm glad to hear it, Reverend," Kristina said, smiling sadly. "Do you want me to play at the funeral?"

"Of course! Do you know any hymns she liked?"

"Samantha and I were not friends," Kristina admitted, crimping her lips. "I have no idea what she did or didn't like. How about if I talk to Allison and get back to you? She's closest to Wesley since they used to be betrothed."

Cody winced again. "Is...why..." He fumbled to a halt.

"Yes, the engagement ended when Wesley married Samantha. Yes, it hurt Allison very much. And yes, they are still close friends. It's best not to ask anything else about those circumstances."

Cody gulped and immediately refocused the conversation as she said, "When should we have the funeral?"

"I think on Saturday would be best. Will they be able to dig her grave in this weather?"

Kristina bobbed her head. "I think so. The ground's cold, but it's not frozen yet."

"Kristina?"

"Yes?"

"Can you get the Ladies' Altar Guild to order some flowers? Is there a budget for funerals?"

"There is. And yes, of course. I'll ask right away."

"Thank you." He reached across the space between them and patted her hand "I suppose it's no surprise my first official ceremony as pastor would be a funeral. I was hoping for a wedding. I like weddings." He made a rueful face.

"Everyone likes weddings, but there's more power in a funeral. I know you can do it, Cody. You're a gifted speaker."

"Thank you."

We're using each other's first names, he realized. It felt right, so he didn't protest it.

Cody and Kristina remained in the corner, quietly making plans for the funeral and supporting Wesley with their presence.

At last, a knock sounded at the door, signaling the arrival of the undertaker. Wesley still sat in a stupor on the sofa, so Cody led them up the stairs to the bedroom, where they began the grim task of preparing Samantha Davis Fulton for burial.

Chapter Six

K ristina and Cody worked together to prepare the nicest funeral Garden City had ever seen. Samantha was ushered to her final resting place with a warmer welcome than she'd ever received while alive, which was a shame, but Cody had arrived too late to do anything more for her.

Finally alone, having just returned from the graveside, he stood at his pulpit overlooking the church. The Ladies' Altar Guild had ordered red mums from down south—which had arrived by overnight train—and a bouquet of white roses for the burial. The flowers had surrounded the simple pine box in which Samantha lay waiting to be interred, washed and dressed in her favorite blue satin, her long blond hair attractively styled, but her face gray and slack.

Cody had preached over the stranger—using information he'd been provided but did not know personally—about how her mental anguish was over. He had heard murmurings of suicide all over town, so he told the congregation that in his opinion, someone whose mind was so disturbed probably lacked the knowledge to be held accountable. He didn't know if he believed it. He had no idea how disturbed Samantha had been, but he took it on faith his friends were telling him the truth and said it anyway. Wesley, it was clear, took comfort in it.

In a way, the tragedy had cemented the friendship between the two men. Talking about his marriage with someone who had never known Samantha seemed to do Wesley some good. Cody offered no recriminations for being seduced by an easy woman, nor did he express disbelief that love, respect and concern could exist between the couple. Cody had listened but said little, allowing Wesley to voice his grief.

He also shared a few pointed opinions Cody wasn't sure he was ready to hear.

Now Wesley finally had gone home. His mother had dragged him away from the graveside while he protested he wasn't ready to go.

In the privacy of his mind, with many prayers of confession, Cody admitted to himself the woman was a battle-ax of the first order. *I'm so glad my mother is a sweet, gentle woman who never barked orders or shoved at my friends.*

Cody's eyes fell on the spot where the casket had lain. *Kristina was right about the power of a funeral service,* he reflected. *My message generated lots of sniffling and digging for handkerchiefs, which people like at a funeral. And then she took over, eliciting more tears and engendering more hope from her seat on the organ bench.*

The highlight had been the choir. On Wednesday night Kristina had taken one look at Cody's exhausted face and ordered him into a chair in the choir loft with a book of music. During a single two-hour practice, the choir had mastered "Abide with Me" in one of her fancy arrangements. When they'd sung it over the body of Samantha Fulton, whatever dry eyes remained in the church had sprung leaks.

I must admit Kristina is a far better choir director than I am.

Kristina. Through the preparations for the funeral, they'd worked closely together. As expected, Wesley didn't want to think about his wife's burial service and had merely trusted his friends to do what was right by her. So, it had been up to the pastor and his organist to put the service together. While the Ladies' Altar Guild had decorated the church, they'd sat together on the pew and chosen hymns, the choir anthem and the opening and closing music.

Her suggestions were fantastic, and I didn't disagree with a single one. As they talked about the content of the sermon, the hymnal in her brain had automatically selected the best pieces. *If we'd been planning something less sad, it would have been enjoyable.* But though Kristina no longer smoldered with rage and resentment, the distance between them remained. *We're colleagues, not friends, and for the life of me, I still can't understand why.*

"It's time to put a stop to this, man," he told himself firmly. "Women like to talk, so talk to her. Find out what you did to upset her and apologize. Make it right. You want to her for a friend. Be a friend. Make the first move."

But what do I say to a woman I've managed to offend three times in a three-week acquaintance, without having the first clue what I did wrong? His internal vehemence startled him, and he blinked, realizing what he was telling himself. *Just why is it so important to be close to Kristina? What do I want from her?*

The answer dawned. *That sparkling, unreserved smile she gave you a couple of times, for starters.*

Cody didn't feel ready to pursue the question of why he wanted the smile. Instead, he stepped down from the pulpit and knelt at the altar to pray.

Kristina lingered at the graveside with Allison far too long. Dusk spread fingers of blackness down towards the hazy orange sunset on the horizon. The chill of the day began to give way to the icy grip of night, and ominous clouds crawled across the sky, crashing into each from one horizon to the other.

"Honey, it wasn't your fault," Kristina told her for the hundredth time. "No one expected you to like and accept her. Remember, she's always been unstable. She was born with something wrong with her. As for the rest... well... I don't know, but no one blames you. Not Wesley, not me, not anyone, so stop blaming yourself. Now come on, let's get you home. It's looking like bad weather."

Allison possessed an impressive height, and she tried to resist, but Kristina had a good two inches on her. She used her size ruthlessly to maneuver her friend away from the grave and down the street to her home.

Allison lived with her parents and sister in a two-story red brick house with carefully tended rose bushes in the front yard and a wrought-iron fence crowned with sharp, dagger-like finials.

Kristina steered Allison through the gate and up to the door, where she knocked. Allison's older sister Becky opened the door and peered out. "Allie, what's wrong?" she asked, and Kristina offered a brief prayer of thanks that her best friend's sister was a kind soul who didn't engage in petty rivalries.

"The funeral upset her," Kristina explained. "Can you get her some tea and make sure she's not left alone for a while?"

"Of course. I know just what to do," Becky insisted. She reached out and clasped Kristina's gloved hand before wrapping her arms around her sister and pulling her into the house.

Alone in the street, Kristina studied the sky again. *It looks like... rain. Rain is bad. Very bad.* Though the temperature hovered barely above freezing, it would change in the next hour. Rain would turn to ice as it fell. She had the entire length of town to cross to get home. Six long blocks. It didn't seem like much, but with the frigid wind whipping down the street between the houses, no coat on earth would keep her warm.

She stepped out from under the Spencers' porch and headed to the corner. Just as she reached Main Street, the heavens opened and a deluge of half-liquid, half-frozen slush pelted down on her.

Thunder growled through the sky, and a flash of lightning lit up the thick, milling clouds overhead.

Kristina began to run.

A crack of thunder startled Cody from his prayers. He crossed to the door and opened it a crack. The wind snatched it from his hand and slammed it into the opposite wall.

Outside, little needles of silver streaked from the sky, slamming to the ground but not splashing. Instead, they coated the street and the lawns in a shimmering layer he could tell was dangerous. Luckily, he only had fifteen steps to get home, so he could afford to wait a bit longer.

Stepping into the frigid blast, he grasped the door firmly and wrestled it shut before returning to the altar and kneeling again.

The temperature was dropping faster than Kristina had predicted. Or maybe it just felt that way because she was soaked to the bone. The wind howled and pushed against her, trying to prevent her from reaching her destination. *I should have stayed with the Spencers. I should stop at any of the homes along the street here and ask for shelter. No one will refuse me.*

Sheer stubbornness kept her moving. *I don't want to borrow some shorter woman's dress and sleep sitting up in a rocking chair by the fire. I want my own home, my own bed. I can still make it.*

The driving wind gusted, nearly knocking her from her feet. She had to grip the trunk of a slender, adolescent oak tree to keep her balance.

You're being stupid, Kristina, to stay out in this. You know how dangerous ice storms can be. People die in them every year. Do you want to be one of those? Do you want the next funeral Cody performs to be yours?

Thoughts of her comfortable bed kept her moving forward despite the voice of reason screaming in her brain. *I can beat this. I will make it home.*

She reached the intersection and crossed the street diagonally. The church was a block down, her home five blocks past it. *I can make it.*

The temperature dropped. She could feel it happening. The driving drizzle changed to blowing snow. Now, compounding the coating of ice on the walkway, visibility had faded to almost nothing. She sucked in a despairing lungful of air as her heart began to pound.

The coldest wind yet shot straight through her sodden coat and scarf, chilling her trembling flesh. She was growing numb and sleepy. *I'll never make it home in this. I'm too far away and it's too cold. I need shelter.* In her mind, shelter became church. Her safe place.

She couldn't see the steeple through the blizzard, but she knew it lay ahead. Only by following the line between street and grass—still just barely visible under its gleaming covering of ice—was she able to stay on course. Step after treacherous, slippery step she made her way until the corner rose to meet her.

"Did I fall?" she wondered aloud. "Why am I on the ground? No matter. I can sleep here. It's growing warmer. I'm quite comfortable."

No! The stubborn German woman inside her screamed. *Don't sleep here, you fool! Get inside the church!*

She tried to stand but found it impossible. She just wanted to rest for a moment, but her stubbornness wouldn't allow it. Cursing the part of herself that forced her, on hands and knees, to make her way to the front of the church, she fumbled along the façade until she found the steps and began to crawl up. At the front door, she rallied enough strength to haul herself upright and pull. The door did not open.

Defeated, Kristina fell against it with a heavy thump.

Inside, another loud sound shook Cody from his prayers. *The thunder is terrible.* He glanced at a transparent portion of the window featuring Elijah and groaned. He'd waited too long. A blizzard howled outside, and he'd never be able to make it to the cozy vicarage. The path twisted too much. *Looks like I'll be spending the night at the church. It's a nuisance, but not too horrible. There's a good supply of firewood near the stove and some food left over from the funeral on the back table. The pews have cushions on them, which, if not as comfortable as a bed, should be decent to sleep on, this once.*

But where's the lightning that accompanied the thunder? I didn't notice a flash, and it seems to me the sound had come, not from the sky, but from the...

Cody's eyes widened. "The Door!" He ran down the aisle and wrestled it open. Sure enough, a figure crouched outside, still as death, not even shivering. He grabbed the person and pulled him inside, shutting out the night and the storm.

Cody pulled the unknown individual to the stove.

"Are you all right?" he asked, but he received no reply. He began unwinding the scarf wrapped around the person's head and face. The fabric had been saturated with water, which had then frozen. Ice cracked and fell, shattering against the floor as he pried the scarf loose.

Tossing the knitted rectangle away, he looked down in horror at the blue-lipped face of Kristina Heitschmidt. The skin between her freckles was desperately pale and tinged with gray. He cupped her face in his hands. Icy. Removing his palms from her cheeks, he sucked in an alarmed breath at the sight of white circles in the center of each one.

They told me that's a sign of frostbite—and the toes and fingers get it the worst. Lord, she won't want to live without her fingers. Please let them not be damaged. Cody lifted one of the long cushions from the pew beside the stove and laid it out on the floor as close to the warmth as he could. Then he tugged Kristina onto it so the heat could thaw her frozen face while he peeled off her gloves. They were also soaked and coated with ice, but the fingers inside remained flexible. *Thank you, God.*

He unbuttoned her sodden coat and slid it from her body, tossing it over the back of the pew.

"Kristina," he said, touching her face again. She gave no sign she'd heard him at all. He grasped her shoulders and gave her a gentle shake. "Kristina, wake up." Nothing, and the sleeves of her shirtwaist felt like they'd been dipped in the river. *This is no time for propriety. She'll catch her death in this wet fabric.*

He worked the buttons hastily, relieved to discover the chemise underneath merely felt damp. Her soaked skirt, soggy shoes, and wet stockings met the same fate. He hung the wet fabric on the backs of the pews and promptly forgot about it. Then he returned to his unexpected companion. She wore only the chemise and a pair of knee-length bloomers, and a shiver shook her. He leaned close to examine her cheeks again. They bloomed bright red with windburn, but the white patches had disappeared.

With a silent prayer of thanks, he urged her down onto the cushion and joined her, wrapping his arms around her body and pulling her onto his lap. She moved like a sleepwalker, clearly unaware of what was happening.

Cody held Kristina, warming her back with his body while the stove radiated heat across her front. Eventually, she began melting into him. Her head fell back against his shoulder, and he couldn't resist the opportunity to let his lips touch her cheek. An aroma of roses wafted from her throat. He kissed her again. Her cinnamon-sprinkled skin felt deliciously soft under his lips.

"Cody?"

Oh good. She's starting to wake up. "Yes, Kristina. I'm here. What were you doing outside in a blizzard?"

"I... I was taking Allison home. She's having a hard time."

"Allison is? Why?"

Kristina remained silent so long, Cody thought she might have truly fallen asleep. He was about to shake her when she drew in a deep breath and spoke. "Guilt. She was jealous of Samantha, always. She wanted Wesley for herself. Now Samantha is dead."

"I see," Cody said, considering. "Why didn't Wesley marry Allison in the first place? Before he could be swayed by... other women?"

"His mother hates her."

Cody sighed. *There are certainly a lot of unpleasant undercurrents in this town.*

"Cody? Where are we?" Her voice sounded slurred and unsteady.

"The church."

"It's late. I have to get home."

"Kristina, you can't. There's a terrible snowstorm outside. You almost didn't make it here. You can't leave until it lets up."

She wriggled out of his arms and stood, weaving as she made her slow way over to the window and looked out. He had never watched a woman walk around in her underwear before, and Kristina wore no corset. The reaction of his body was immediate and painful.

Her shoulders sagged. "It's not going to let up," she said at last, her voice a study in misery.

"Are you sure?"

"I've lived here my whole life. This kind of blizzard won't blow out until morning.

Cody understood the implications. The inevitability of their future together both thrilled and worried him. "Kristina, you know what that means?"

She stepped closer to the window. He could no longer see her face, but her arms came up around herself, and her shoulders began shaking.

Realizing she was crying, he went to her and swept her into his arms for a tight hug before leading her back to the stove. "Come on, Kristina. Stay here. Might as well be warm if nothing else." He sat down on the cushion and pulled her back into his lap.

She squirmed uncomfortably, rubbing against the part of him that was poking into her hip.

"Sorry," he said, easing her away from him. "Now, can you tell me why you're so upset? Am I really such a bad prospect as to be worth all those tears?"

She wrestled for control for several movements before she was able to answer. "Yes." The word emerged choked and almost incomprehensible, but Cody understood, and it stung him straight to the heart.

"Why? What happened between us? I thought we were getting along, becoming friends. What happened to make you so angry with me?"

She mumbled something he couldn't hear.

He cuddled her closer. "What was that?"

"You stole my life."

"What? What do you mean? I don't understand." Little bubbles of anger stirred in his belly, but he squashed them.

She shook her head. "It doesn't matter."

"It does. 'Till death do us part' is a long time to live with someone who resents you. Tell me, so I can try to fix it."

"It's a long story."

"We have all night."

She turned to look at him consideringly over her shoulder. "I never planned to marry," she began. "When I was younger, I used to hate my looks because I knew no man would ever want me for a wife. Too tall. Too ugly."

Her eyes lingered on his face. "At one time I wrestled with it, but then I came to realize there were other ways to live. I'm blessed with a gift, so while a family was not in my future, I could have a career. I could play music and make people happy. It was a good calling and helped me make peace with my appearance. I was accepted to the music school, and it was so exciting. I learned new techniques, more difficult pieces. I learned to arrange music, and even write it. And I was good, Cody."

She turned partway in his embrace so he could see her turquoise eyes as they flashed in the light of the stove. "Best in my class. Better than the boys. I traveled, played in churches all over Kansas, and into Missouri and Iowa. I was making a name for myself. It would have been a glorious life. I was so looking forward to my last year of classes, and then the big world out there. New York, San Francisco, even Europe. It was all laid out before me."

Her storytelling tone faded into one of dejection, shoulders sagging. "And then the cholera came to town. Everyone got sick. Children, adults, old people. The pastor of the church and the sheriff. Mom too. Dad locked up the store and tried to take care of her, but... she didn't make it. Her illness and death drained the finances Dad needed to pay for my schooling. Then my brother disappeared. I couldn't leave Dad alone with his grief, and there was no money left for school anyway, so I gave up my studies and stayed home. A melancholy settled over me then. I grew sadder and sadder. That's when the elder board came to me. They said without a regular pastor, with them taking turns preaching, there would be no church music. They asked me to help out. It was just what I needed."

"How on earth did everyone get their minds around a woman —let alone such a young woman— leading? Didn't the pronouncement ruffle any feathers?" Cody wanted to know.

She dipped her chin in a brief nod. "Yes. But the elders told them I had their complete support. Only two left the choir because I was leading it, and when the music started to get better and better, one came back. So, I no longer had a concert career to look forward to, but I still had a purpose. This is my service to the Lord, the church, and the community. I can't decorate, my sewing skills are poor, and I'll never have children to fill the pews, but I can still contribute something. This gives my life meaning. Or it did, until..." she trailed off.

Cody closed his eyes. "Until I came and took it away from you."

"Yes."

"Why didn't you say anything?" He asked, tenderly stroking his hand over her cheek. *Her skin is so soft.*

"I did, Cody," she protested, even as she allowed the touch. "I told you I was territorial about the music. You didn't listen."

"And I took away your purpose."

"Yes."

"I'm sorry, Kristina," he said. "You're right. I didn't listen. I assumed... well in my old church, all the women complained when they were asked to serve."

"Every woman?" She raised one russet eyebrow.

Cody thought back. "No. I remember a lot of complaining, but now you mention it, there were several who contributed eagerly."

"You see?" she demanded.

"I do now. Well, it's easy to fix. The choir doesn't want me anyway. They only want you. And, well, we can work together planning out the services. It will be easy now."

"Cody, do we really have to..."

"Yes," he insisted. "I won't have us gossiped about. Besides, you're sitting in my lap in your underwear. That's pretty thoroughly compromised, no matter how much of a gentleman I am."

She tried to escape but he held her tight. "Don't go, Kristina. It's too late, so we might as well enjoy it."

Her eyes widened.

A prickling sensation of heat spread slowly up his neck onto his cheeks. "Not like that. I meant enjoy the warmth. I won't take advantage of you, so just relax, and let me hold you. Think, darlin', how convenient it will be, the two of us together. We can work on services whenever we want, and you'd have my backing and support for your music. I promise I won't meddle anymore. I'll ask what you want instead of assuming. We'll work together as a team. Is it okay, Kristina?"

"So, you're proposing a marriage of convenience then?"

Why does she sound so sad? Hopeful her tone meant what he thought it might, he responded, "No. I'm proposing a marriage. The fact it's convenient is nice, but if we're going to be together, it'll be for real."

"Oh. Um, I don't know anything about that." He could almost feel her blush.

"Neither do I," he admitted, "but we'll work it out. Now then, I would like something from you."

"What's that?"

In lieu of an answer, he took her shoulders in his hands and turned her to face him.

"Cody, what?" was all she managed to say before his mouth captured hers. He had noticed her lips when they first met. He'd thought them pretty then. Now, mashed under his, he found them wonderful; soft, full and utterly delicious. He kissed her once, a hard, brief peck, and then raised his head. Even in the dim light of the flickering lamps, he could see her turquoise eyes, the pupils dilated with the dark and her own awakening desire.

"Cody?" Her voice sounded so tentative, he kissed her again. She remained passive against his onslaught of passionate embraces. His lips brushed hers, trailed across her cheeks, her forehead, the tip of her nose. A dam of confused, powerful feelings burst forth inside Cody and he poured them over her in a flood of kisses, at last ending back at her mouth.

This time, Kristina pursed her lips in welcome. He felt the moment her will softened, and he pressed, tonguing the seam and asking for more. She let him in and inhaled sharply through her nose as he tasted her.

At last, Cody could take no more stimulation. He released her mouth, though his arms around her remained tight.

"What was that?" she asked, bewildered.

"Us sealing our engagement with a kiss," he replied, stating the obvious. "I think you can see it will be no hardship for me to be married to you."

She blinked, confusion warring with languorous passion.

"Kristina, darlin', let go of the idea you're undesirable. There's so much more to attraction than looks. There's nothing wrong with yours, but besides beauty, there's the whole woman inside."

"But my freckles..."

He regarded the little spots with growing heat. "I want to kiss every one of them. After the wedding, I will."

Her cheeks darkened. He touched his lips to her blush.

She looked unconvinced. *Lord, help me reassure this woman.*

It had struck Cody before that when he prayed for unselfish things, he received a lavish response. Words he would never have thought of spilled from him.

"Take Miss Jackson, for instance. She's beautiful to look at, but every time she opens her mouth, the ugliness of her spirit pours out. Her beauty doesn't tempt me. She leaves me cold. Why? Because she's selfish and cruel. I look at you and, yes I see your freckles and your red hair."

He smoothed a disheveled strawberry strand off her forehead. "But I also see you struggling through the cold with food for me. I see you playing the organ at the funeral of a woman who was not your friend and trying your level best to make it the performance of a lifetime. You have a generous spirit, Kristina. It tempts me. As do your sweet lips." He ran a finger over the rosy, well-kissed Cupid's bow. "And your eyes. I love your eyes. They remind me of home, with all the depth and color of the Gulf of Mexico. We could make a home together, Kristina. Don't you want to?"

Her eyes met his, the gaze as intense as their previous embraces had been. He could see her innermost thoughts as though she'd spoken the words aloud. *Do I dare to hope? Will I be able to have the family I never imagined? A husband who respects and cares for me. My purpose back.* And then her eyes darkened. *It isn't by choice. We got trapped here overnight. He'd never be doing this if not for the storm—the odd set of circumstances aligned just right to force us together.*

"That's not true, you know," he told her.

She raised one eyebrow in silent question.

"I was going to talk to you anyway... next week, after the service. I was going to find out what was wrong and try to make it right. I wanted to... see if I could get back those... good feelings that were growing between us before I put my foot in my mouth so badly. It seems likely this would have been the result anyway. The only thing the storm changes is the timing."

Doubt as bold as the blizzard darkened her expression. *She doesn't believe me. And why should she? This is all happening far too fast. How long have we known each other? Three weeks? Four? Not nearly enough.* Cody risked his self-control for one more sweet kiss on her full-lipped mouth. No tongue, because his battered self-control wouldn't take it, but a tender smudge of his lips across hers.

She'll learn to trust me if I'm careful with her. And I will be. Lord help me woo this woman. A sense of peace and rightness soothed Cody. *There are no accidents in the Divine plan. I'm here, and so is she, for this reason. The storm arose when it did for this reason.*

Cody smiled. There must have been something telling in that smile because Kristina's eyes widened. He touched his lips to her forehead and then urged her down on the cushion. Rising, he walked across the sanctuary and retrieved one lamp from the pulpit, extinguishing the other. Then he entered the storage room. A few minutes of rummaging brought to light a long, white robe. He imagined it was used for Christmas Pageant angels.

He carried the garment back to where she lay and handed it to her. She sat and slipped it over her head. It was loosely cut and covered her to mid-calf. She was shivering, he saw, in the absence of his warmth, and he poked at the thick woolen stockings draped over the arm of the nearby pew. Dry and warm. Perfect. He brought them to her, and she pulled them on. Decently if oddly covered, she lay down again. Cody joined her, draping his arm over the curve of her waist.

"Try to sleep, darlin'. There's going to be nothing but big days for quite a while."

She nodded. He touched his lips to the side of her neck. She snuggled against him so every inch of her body curved into his. She felt perfect there, comfortable and right.

Cody gripped Kristina tighter, and peace enveloped the couple.

Chapter Seven

While the couple slumbered in the warmest corner of the church, the storm blew itself out.

Just before sunrise, alarmed his daughter had not returned home, James Heitschmidt bundled himself heavily against the cold and walked across town to Allison Spencer's house. He knocked on the door with precipitous urgency.

A moment later, Allison poked her head out. The young spinster's eyes looked red and heavy, and dark circles marred the tanned skin underneath. "Mr. Heitschmidt, what's going on?"

"Kristina didn't come home last night," he blurted. "Did she stay here?"

"No." Allison shook her head vigorously. "She brought me home from the funeral and left again."

"Did she say anything?" he demanded. "Did she give any indication of... uh... umm...?"

Behind Allison, a small, slim figure had moved into view, and James's questioning stuttered to a halt.

"She didn't say anything, Mr. Heitschmidt. I'm sorry," Rebecca's soft, serene voice held more than a tinge of concern. "Dear Lord, I hope she wasn't caught out in that."

James nodded, swallowed the lump in his throat, and

said, "I'm not going to rest until I find her." Then he squeezed his eyes shut. *Stupid thing to say. As if I would. Lord, I wish I could talk like a normal man in front of Rebecca Spencer.*

"Of course not," Allison insisted, grabbing a coat and dragging it on, "and neither will we, right, Becky?"

Becky responded with a curt nod, already reaching for her own outerwear. "Let's start at Lydia's. It's about halfway, and we've all stayed over there at one time or another. Plus, with that stove always going, it's nice and warm inside."

"Good idea," James agreed.

The three of them hurried down the sidewalk to the café and ducked through the dining room into the kitchen.

Lydia, up early as always, paused from her stew making and bread baking to regard her unexpected guests with curiosity.

"Did Kristina stay with you last night?" Allison demanded without preamble.

The curvaceous chef's face paled. "No, I haven't seen her since the graveside. Why?" She gulped, clearly already knowing the answer.

"She never made it home," James told her anyway. "I had hoped she stopped here."

"I wish she had," Lydia replied. "Do let me know when you find her, won't you?"

"Of course," Becky told her friend as they bundled out the door.

In the street, the chill had lessened to a faint coolness, though the ice on the ground remained treacherous.

"Now what?" James demanded, panic setting in. Snow piled on the lawns high enough to bury a woman. If Kristina had perished in the storm, she would not be found until it melted.

A soft pressure on his arm drew his attention from his inward despair to Rebecca Spencer's lovely, light eyes. "Kristina is a bright young woman. She wouldn't linger in the cold and die. Somewhere along this street, she's holed up snug and warm. We just have to figure out where. Let's walk along the route and see if we can find her."

He allowed her to lead him away from the café. As they made their way down the street, he pondered each house and business in turn.

The mercantile would make sense, but I have the only key at home. The bank was all closed up. She wasn't close to the Robinsons or the Jacksons. The light of the sun hit the steeple of the church, casting a shadowy cross over him. "What if she sought refuge inside?" he asked, indicating the building.

Allison nodded. "I bet that's just what she did. Let's look."

James pulled out his keyring and fumbled, fingers shaking with cold, until he could fit the key into the church's lock, only to realize, upon jiggling, that his effort would not be needed. The unlocked door swung open and the Spencers and Kristina's father slipped inside. The warmth from the stove drew them to the corner.

No one could have predicted the sight that met their eyes. Kristina, dressed like a Christmas angel slept on a pew cushion. The young pastor warmly embraced her.

James drew an unsteady breath. *I know my daughter, and I trust her. I think I know Cody, too. This was an accident, not a seduction, and I'd bet my life on my daughter's virtue still being intact. But the damage to her reputation will be inevitable, and the outcome is obvious.*

A strange mixture of grief and joy blended in James's heart. *If anyone can give my daughter the marriage she deserves, it's Cody Williams.* But like any father, the thought of handing his child over to a man caused a deep pang.

"Kristina." He touched her arm gently. Her eyes opened, and the expression in them was one of deep contentment.

And then tranquility turned to a vibrant blush that matched her hair as she realized what everyone was seeing.

"Dad, I..."

"It's all right, honey. I'm just glad you're safe."

Their voices awakened Cody, and for just a heartbeat of time, James saw his arms tighten protectively around Kristina's slender waist. Then he released her.

"Better get dressed, darlin'," Cody told her. "It's Sunday morning, and the congregation will be here any moment. You need to get home and change. It won't do for you still to be wearing what you wore to the funeral."

Kristina, her blush even redder than before, nodded and gathered up her stiff, unpleasant clothing, scampering into the office to change.

Left alone with the man who had ruined his daughter, James found himself struck dumb with awkwardness.

"Sir," Cody began, "I know how it looked, but I swear..."

"I know." James held up both hands. "I know you didn't take advantage of her. She wouldn't have let you anyway."

Cody babbled over him. "We were just trying to stay warm and..."

James grasped the nervous young pastor's shoulder. "I understand, Reverend. Calm down. I'm not angry, but you know what this means."

"Of course. We talked it all out last night." Cody's mouth curled upwards in one corner. "I think we would have gotten here eventually anyway."

"I do too. Anyone who could make Kristina that mad had to have a special place in her heart." James sighed. "So, at any rate, you'll join us for lunch today, so we can make plans." It wasn't a request.

Cody nodded.

"You'd better head home, Reverend," James urged. "You don't want to be seen in your funeral clothes either."

Cody's grin turned sheepish. "Cody, please. We're almost family, right?"

James sighed. "Okay."

Kristina emerged, interrupting the awkward exchange. Cody went straight to her as though drawn by a magnet. Ignoring the small crowd standing by, he took her hand in his and kissed her cheek. "I'm going now. Will you be back for the service?"

"Of course. Will you make the announcement?" He could see uncertainty in her turquoise eyes.

Sweet, hesitant Kristina. Believe in this. It's real as we are. "Yes. I'll let everyone know you've done me the honor of agreeing to be my wife."

"Honor." She looked away, blushing.

"It *is* an honor, Kristina," he told her solemnly. "You're a strong enough woman that you don't need a husband, but you agreed to marry me anyway. I realize what a blessing that is."

She looked back up at him through her eyelashes.

He let heat bleed into his expression. Answering desire flared in hers. Suddenly, inappropriately, he longed for another kiss. *Soon*, he reminded himself. *Soon she'll be my wife and I can kiss her all night long.* It was the wrong thought, and he had to release her and leave the church quickly before anyone could realize what had just happened.

"Well, Kristina," She looked up at her father in silence, "this is quite a predicament you've gotten yourself into. What were you doing out in the storm?"

"Trying to get home," she replied mildly.

"You should have stayed with the Spencers," he scolded, but he was smiling.

Kristina's confused emotions made his expression impossible to decipher. Shaking her head, she walked past her father toward the door. Before she could get outside, though, Allison scooped her into a tight hug, almost crushing her ribs. "I'm so glad you're okay," she said. "I was worried. I mean, with Samantha and all, I..."

At last, Kristina found her voice. "I know, I'm sorry. I wasn't thinking. I just wanted to get home."

"And now?" Allison pressed.

Kristina thought of Cody. *What a handsome man, and he's my man. What a concept.* Yet try though she might to reason it away, the undeniable truth stood firm as the church itself. He'd kissed her and held her all through the night. *Soon he'll be my...* her mind veered away from the word. *I'm not ready to deal with all the implications yet, but I, plain, freckle-faced Kristina Heitschmidt, have a suitor. A betrothed. It's beyond belief.* A slow smile spread across her face. "Now I think things are going to be all right."

Then she squeezed Allison and turned to hug Becky before heading out into the cold. *Cold? It isn't so very cold after all.* The sun sparkling on the snow had a strength Kristina hadn't expected so soon after a blizzard. At this rate, it would all melt in no time. She rolled her eyes.

Kristina hurried through the mushy, leftover precipitation, soaking her still-damp boots even further, and arrived at home quickly. Amazing to think the same distance had almost killed her less than twelve hours ago.

She stepped through the door, removing her wet footwear and leaving it on the porch. In damp stockings, she made her way to the stairs and climbed up to her room.

Her heart pounded from the swift ascent. As she stepped into the room, the heavy reality of the night and all it meant broke over her. She slumped against the wall beside the door and breathed slowly, taking in the familiar details of her bedroom to calm her nerves.

Like the rest of the house, it had been decorated simply. A black quilt covered the brass-framed bed against the far wall. Above it hung a simple painting of a piano.

A lacquered hope chest stood at the foot of the bed, unadorned except for its brass finishes. Her bedside table was also black with scarlet flowers painted on the surface. A wardrobe stood in one corner of the room. A vanity table with a wash basin had been placed in the opposite corner.

The church bell chimed, making Kristina jump. *I have to get ready.* While there was nothing she would like better at this moment than to relive Cody's kisses again and again, she had to get back to the church. The service was starting, and she still wore the stiff, damp funeral clothes. Quickly she stripped off her skirt and shirtwaist, bloomers and chemise, and her still-damp stockings. Nude, she crossed to the vanity and washed her face in the chilly water. Her oversized mirror reflected her body to the waist.

The sight of her bare breasts gave her a moment's pause. *Marriage means... certain things. I'm not sure I'm ready for them.* While she understood the mechanics—stray cats and dogs were not subtle in their coupling—it was different with people. *Especially as the person in question is me. I'll have to undress and let him see me. Let him see my freckled breasts and belly, hips and legs. There isn't a part of me that lacks these blasted spots.*

The bell tolled again, and she hurried to the wardrobe and pulled out clean undergarments, which she donned with all due haste. Then a coffee-colored skirt and a white shirtwaist. Returning to the dresser, she dragged a brush through her waves of sunset hair, twirling it into a bun and pinning it as fast as she could. One strand escaped, tickling the back of her neck, but there was no time to fix it. She found a pair of black boots in the bottom of her wardrobe and shoved her feet into them despite them being pinchingly uncomfortable. Last, she tossed a cream-colored shawl with long fringes and embroidered pink flowers around her shoulders.

Forgoing her damp coat, she ran back down the street to the church. The pew had been reassembled in her absence, and no sign remained of the improper night she'd spent cradled in Cody's arms. She couldn't help but glance at the stove as she hurried up the stairs to the organ, trying not to stomp her boots on the treads. The congregation had begun singing without her. Rather than playing in the middle of the song, she let them carry on *a cappella*.

After the opening hymn came announcements, prayer requests, and church business. Cody read through the list. Mrs. Jones had a cough. Ethel and Lowell's baby had been born large and healthy last week. Mother and child were doing well. There would be a meeting of the Ladies' Altar Guild Tuesday night. The Christmas cantata was only two weeks away.

And then Cody dropped his bombshell.

"Friends, in the brief time I've been here, you've made me feel welcome, and I thank you, but no one has done more to facilitate my integration than Miss Kristina Heitschmidt. Therefore, I have decided to make her a permanent part of my life by marrying her. To my very great surprise, she has agreed."

Silence. And then a gasp as the entire one hundred eighty-six members of the congregation sucked in their breath as one. Kristina grinned.

"No arrangements have been made yet," Cody continued, "but I sincerely hope all of you will wish us well. And now, if you would take your Bibles and turn to Psalm 57. We will read responsively, whole verse by whole verse."

That's the way, she thought. *Don't give them time to start whispering.*

After the reading would be another hymn. Kristina squinted at the board below, trying to make out the numbers, and then flipped silently through the thin pages.

She tried to concentrate on the service, she really did, but it was impossible. Too many radical changes had left her reeling. Plus, she was starving. She hadn't eaten since the funeral the previous afternoon. All she could think about was getting home, so she could make lunch... and share it with Cody. *It's a good thing my back is to him, so he can't see the silly smile on my face.*

The hour dragged by with excruciating slowness, but at last, Kristina played the closing hymn and scurried down the stairs to stand beside Cody as he shook hands with the departing congregation. Of course, in the wake of such momentous news, the leave-taking took twice as long as usual. Despite her gnawing hunger, Cody's hand on her lower back spread warmth through her that had nothing to do with the weak December sunshine.

The last of the congregation departed. Cody took Kristina's arm and they walked together with James beside them down a street now completely clear of the snow. Even the piles on the grass shrank at a seemingly impossible speed.

The warmth made the walk pleasant, though none of them felt like conversing along the way. They mounted the steps to the porch of the Heitschmidt home and entered. Cody didn't seem inclined to wait in the parlor; instead, he followed Kristina into the kitchen.

Kristina prepared a simple lunch of sandwiches—there was no time for anything more elaborate—and Cody helped her carry them into the dining room. James already waited at the head of the table, and they joined him, one on either side, facing each other. Cody asked a brief blessing and the hungry trio devoured several bites of the food before the serious conversation began.

"Well, children," James said, "what are we going to do now?"

"I think we all agree about what needs to be done," Cody replied, grinning at the man who would soon be his father-in-law and reaching across the table to grasp Kristina's hand.

"Yes," she agreed as heat suffused her face.

"Oh, I know that." James dismissed their comments with a wave. "But when?"

"Soon," Cody said. "Right away. We all know nothing improper happened, but the fact is, Kristina and I spent the night alone together. It can't be changed. So, the sooner the deed is done, the better."

"I agree," Kristina seconded. "Before Christmas, if we can swing it."

"That soon?" James asked, eyes wide.

"I think the Friday before," Kristina said. "The Cantata is next Sunday, so that will give us almost a week afterwards."

"It's still not much time," James commented. "Will you be able to get ready by then? I don't like the thought of a small, thrown-together wedding for my only daughter."

"Dad," she protested, "until yesterday, I never thought of having a wedding at all. I'm not interested in a lot of expensive fanciness. You know I like things simple."

"That is true," he agreed, looking around the plain, unadorned dining room.

A flutter of anxiety squirmed through her belly. "Cody, that won't bother you, will it?" She turned her eyes on him, her expression beseeching. "I can keep body and soul together well enough, but I don't like to spend time creating and maintaining a lot of dust-catchers. I guess I'm only marginally domestic."

Taking her concerns seriously, Cody's eyes scanned the room and then returned to hers. "Bother me? No, not at all. There's something fitting about a pastor's household looking simple. It suggests we spend our time on more meaningful pursuits. Honestly, Kristina, I don't care in the slightest about doilies."

One corner of her mouth turned upwards. He lifted her hand to his lips and kissed a patch of freckles adorning the little space between her thumb and forefinger. A sizzle of heat obliterated the nervous flutter.

James observed the interaction between his daughter and this near-stranger who would soon be her husband. *It seems likely they'll be a good match. There's an easy affection between them. The tension and animosity of the past weeks are melting with the snow. Now they look like any courting couple. Enamored, shy, and eager to please. But they still don't know each other well, and there's next to no time to learn more.*

She returned to her lunch, but instead of tearing hungrily at her sandwich, she began nibbling daintily.

The pastor devoured his sandwich and helped himself to another from the platter, but his eyes never left Kristina.

James grinned. *He looks like a fish being slowly reeled in, and the best part is, she has no idea she's reeling. It's not a game for them. These two genuinely care about each other. They're pulling closer; an affinity of personalities and souls that will make for quite a satisfying union. Trudy and I were like that. Just easy, caring about the same kinds of things. I miss her.*

He shook off the thought of his late wife, cleared his throat and, seeing that the sandwich plate lay empty, spoke again. "All right then. Get yourselves some more coffee and let's go sit in the parlor. We have some more to discuss."

Kristina and Cody glanced at each other, but gamely poured themselves mugs of the hot beverage and walked arm-in-arm down the hallway to the parlor. The couple sat together on the sofa. Not one speck of ebony fabric showed between their legs.

Cody took Kristina's hand in his and set it on his knee. James noted how her eyes dropped to see where Cody touched her, and a faint pinkness stained her cheeks. Her lips curved, and she returned her gaze to eye level, but that hint of a pleased smile lingered. James swallowed hard. *Much as I know it's good and right, it still hurts to think of her leaving.*

Again, James pushed forward, using conversation to dispel lingering melancholy. "As I see it, there's one main problem. Gossip. There's no way to prevent people from talking, but are you sure you want to hurry into marriage? A long engagement would go further to demonstrate you have confidence in your innocence."

They looked at each other, and then back at him. Kristina spoke first. "No. I don't want to wait," she said simply.

Cody's thumb rubbed over her knuckle. "Not to mention," he added bluntly, "while I have confidence in our innocence, I'm not entirely certain about my stamina."

James gave his prospective son-in-law a hard-eyed look.

"That's something I don't particularly want to think about," he told him.

Cody shrugged. "Sorry. It's a fact. Now that I've given the idea of marriage some thought, I'd like to get it done."

Just what he was planning to 'get done' didn't sit well with Kristina's father. Rage bubbled in his innards.

No. Suppress the anger. Kristina deserves a husband who desires her. She deserves a real marriage. Let her have that.

James made no further comment on the uncomfortable subject. "Well, if you're both settled, there's nothing more to be said, is there? I hope you don't regret your rush. You know the saying."

"I do." Cody was looking at Kristina again. Her gaze on his burned with a new attraction that matched his.

"Well then," James said, "I'll let you two work out the details. But there is one thing I'm going to insist on. Between now and the wedding, Cody, I expect you to pay a call every night. Kristina's never had a suitor. I won't have her miss out entirely on being courted."

"I have no intention of arguing with that plan," Cody replied.

"And at the end of each visit, I'll give you ten unsupervised minutes, in case you need to talk about anything private."

That, Kristina understood. She drew in an unsteady breath, and her face turned the color of her freckles. "Dad..."

"I think I'd like to get rid of this cup," James told them mildly. "I'll be right back."

He stalked out of the room, his boots clicking on the polished wooden floors. The door banged shut behind him, the sound unnoticed by the couple on the sofa.

"Was he really suggesting..." Kristina began.

"He was," Cody replied, grinning, "and not just in the

evenings either. What do you say, darlin'? You up for another kiss?"

She gave him a wide-eyed look in lieu of words. He took the cup from her hands and set it, and his, on the side table. Then he took her warm, soft cheeks in his hands and lowered his lips to hers in a tender caress.

Cody's obvious desire for her was sweet as candy, heady as wine, and she drank it in. Deep, drowning draughts of affection swept over her, making her feel cherished. As affection slowly gave way to arousal, she went there too, parting her lips at the pressure of his tongue so he could taste her. This time she felt bold enough to taste him back, letting her tongue swipe gently over his.

"Hmmm," Cody hummed into her mouth. His hands left her face and slid around her, crushing her against his chest.

I think I like to be crushed.

He pulled back to look into her eyes from a few devastating inches away. The expression in his evening blue gaze overwhelmed her, and she shamelessly pulled him back for another embrace.

Startled by her aggression, Cody froze, but he quickly thawed, letting her take the lead. This time she slipped her tongue into his mouth.

They spent every second of the ten minutes playing on the safe side of passion. One kiss blended into another, but despite the painful state of his arousal, Cody kept his hands planted firmly on her back. *I won't push. There will be time for everything else later. And not too much later either.*

A tap on the parlor door eventually interrupted their long kiss.

"Time's up," Cody joked, glad he was seated. He took in Kristina's kiss-stung lips and knew there would be no secrets.

He shrugged.

They would be married in less than two weeks. No one would

begrudge them a stolen embrace while her father no doubt waited just on the other side of the door.

James entered. The couple sat hand in hand, just as they had when he'd left them. But now they both drew in heavy breaths, the evidence of their behavior obvious. Though it wasn't wrong, it did bother him.

"Kristina," James said, "I think you should... rest. You had a wild day yesterday and I don't want you to get sick. Cody, I'm glad you came for lunch. We'll see you tomorrow night."

"Thank you for inviting me," the young pastor replied. He squeezed his intended's hand gently, murmured something James couldn't hear and took his leave of them.

Chapter Eight

On Monday, the weather warmed even further. It felt like spring instead of December. As Cody shaved at the sink, the events of the last two days washed over him. He set the razor down, not sure his hands were steady enough to perform the delicate task safely. *I don't want to slit my own throat less than two weeks before my wedding.*

Wedding. In a handful of days, he would be a married man.

Cody swallowed hard. He'd been waiting a long time for this. Now that it was almost upon him, he didn't quite know what to think. He wasn't a eunuch. The desire for intimacy with a woman had been just as strong for him as for anyone, but he hated hypocrisy. There was no way he could, with a clear conscience, promote celibacy and not practice it.

Cody had felt the call to the ministry at the age of ten. He didn't want a secret past to mar his work, so with many prayers, he'd endured the constant burning arousal of adolescence and the intense desire of a previous, failed courtship. Though it had floundered after a couple of months, while that relationship had lasted, Cody had feared he might lose his mind from the unrequited lust.

But he'd endured. Now he faced a different... problem was the wrong word. Situation. Though looking forward to his marriage with Kristina, he had no idea how to handle the physical side of it. There would be one. He'd told her it was not a marriage of convenience, and he had every intention of making it true. Holding her close in his arms on the night of the blizzard had made it abundantly clear to him he would need relief before long, and he would finally be allowed to have it. Well, in ways other than the one his body had taken unbidden in the night.

His mind flashed to a hazy image of Kristina, spread out on the bed wearing only a gold band on her ring finger, and suddenly that spontaneous release no longer sufficed. There had been a reason—entirely apart from gossip and scandal—why he had wanted this marriage and wanted it so quickly.

Ignoring the ache of arousal, Cody dressed quickly. Though Monday was his off from church work, he had a great many things to do.

He decided he would not need his heavy coat. The light one more than sufficed. He added a hat but left off gloves. Then he strode down the street to the commercial part of town.

This was the only street in town that was paved, not simple, hard-packed earth, but in red bricks that matched the buildings.

The towering Occidental Hotel dominated the skyline. Next to it the bank only comprised a single story. Other buildings, made of the same materials but varying in size, lined both sides of the wide brick street. Some sported green and white striped awnings, others had windows lined with white frames. A few had empty window boxes.

Cody made a beeline for an office located in the vestibule of the bank. The glass-fronted cubicle housed a single desk in scarred mahogany, on which rested a black and chrome machine. Nearby, a man with a green visor denting his copious pomade scribbled with a stub of a pencil on a sheet of paper.

Cody entered the bank and made the sharp turn into the telegraph office.

The operator, a young man he had not yet met, finished recording the incoming message and looked up. "Hiya,

Reverend," he said in a nasal twang as he stuck his pencil behind his ear.

"Hello," Cody replied. He almost asked the young man how he knew him, as he hadn't seen him at church. But in a town this size, new arrivals would certainly be noted by all. "I'd like to send a message, please."

The young man pulled out his pencil again. Then he cursed as the machine began clicking, indicating another incoming message.

Holding up a hand to Cody, the operator recorded the new message and sent back the acknowledgment.

"Okay, Reverend, better be quick. It's busy as all get-out today."

Cody grinned. Then he relayed his message, enjoying watching the clerk's eyes bug out at the unexpected information.

"Now you're sure," Cody teased, "this information will be kept confidential? I don't want to have my personal business gossiped about."

The young man went red. Cody could see his guilt for what he would not be able to stop himself from doing.

"I would like the same message sent to Dr. Abraham Thomas at Alexander College in Jacksonville, Texas," he added.

"Yes, sir," the clerk replied. "Right away, Reverend."

Cody paid for the two messages and headed back out into the street. The morning sun hung high overhead. Less than two days after the snowstorm, the piles had been reduced to slushy puddles gathering in the low spots on lawns. A hint of green showed among the brown threads of the grass.

The lovely weather made him want to stay outside, so he walked to the edge of town and cast his eyes across the prairie. The shoulder-high grasses waved in the Kansas wind. One type had tufts of gold as large as a child's palm adorning each stalk. Another modeled light and dark green stripes along the entire length of the blades. Still another towered above the others in thick emerald clumps, the color undimmed by the shortening days.

Among them all, wild sunflowers, their golden petals returned to earth, bowed heavy, brown faces to the ground. He imagined the height of summer, those yellow sunbursts following their namesake from horizon to horizon. *Lord willing, next summer I'll be here to see it, with my wife on my arm.*

My wife. She fits in here, with her golden-red hair like a prairie flower. He would hold her and cover her with indiscreet kisses while the summer sun slipped over the horizon, and then take her back home...

Cody sighed. *I did it again.* How interesting that once the desire for a woman took hold, it consumed every waking moment.

Movement drew his eye. Turning, he saw the object of his consideration standing a few feet away, also staring out across the prairie. Today she wore a turquoise suit that showed off to perfection her curvaceous figure.

She didn't seem to notice him. He wanted her to, so he approached her silently from behind, slipping his arms around her waist.

She must have been aware of his presence because she showed no surprise at his touch. Instead, she leaned her head back against his shoulder. He touched his lips to a patch of little speckles adorning her temple. Then he leaned his chin on her shoulder and looked out to the horizon.

"It feels like the ocean," he commented.

"What do you mean?" she asked softly.

He kissed her temple again. "The prairie. It stretches as far as the eye can see, clear out to the horizon. I always loved to pray beside the ocean. It reminded me how much bigger than me God is if His creation makes me feel so insignificant. And it moves. Always moving."

"So maybe Kansas isn't so different from Galveston after all?"

What's that note of worry in her voice? "I'm not changing my mind, Kristina. I still want to marry you."

"Oh, I know," she replied. "I just worry that eventually Kansas will be too different from Texas, and you'll miss your family and want to leave."

"Well," Cody said slowly, his eyes still on the horizon, enjoying the smooth softness of Kristina's cheek against his, "I would like to visit now and again. I hope you will be willing."

"Of course."

"But I'm an adult now. I don't want to run back to my parents. I've decided Kansas is my home. So long as the Lord keeps me here, I'm content to stay. It's a small town, but there's so much to be done. I feel like I can make a difference in this place."

He felt her skin move and knew it was a smile. A chilly breeze drove her deeper into the cradle of his arms. He held her tenderly.

"Is it wrong that I want to stay here to be close to my dad?" she asked.

"I don't think so," he replied. "My parents have each other, and my older sister and her husband and children live in Austin. They're not alone like your father would be if you left."

She nodded. "That's how I feel too."

"Good," he told her. "We agree. Now then, Kristina, I feel like being indiscreet. Turn around, darlin', and let me kiss you for a while."

She faced him almost before he could finish speaking, slipping her arms around his neck.

"Why, Miss Heitschmidt, do you want to be kissed?" Cody feigned shock.

"Why yes, Reverend Williams. Yes, I do. You must think me a terrible hussy." Her blush told him her teasing tone concealed a real concern.

"A hussy, Miss Heitschmidt?" He maintained the jest but addressed her concern nonetheless. "Of course, you're not a hussy. You're soon to be married. I think you're entitled to desire a few kisses from your future husband."

He lowered his head, giving her his mouth.

It's a mistake, Cody realized quickly, *to kiss her so much*. The longing had passed beyond painful to excruciating, but it didn't matter. Cody kissed Kristina while his body burned and throbbed. He kissed her and felt her lips grow soft and submissive under his. He kissed her and ground his aching sex against her belly.

At last, she pulled back. The sight of her love-pinkened lips nearly destroyed him. *I never understood how passion could take people over and make them forget decency and life-long standards of right and wrong.*

He'd seen it over and over, from King David to members of his former congregation. Now he knew. *Eleven days to my wedding. Days, not months, and the temptation to have her is quickly spiraling out of control.*

"Cody, what's happening?" Kristina asked, sounding shaken, her voice unsteady and weak.

"I want you, darlin'," he told her bluntly. "That's why I didn't want to wait for a spring wedding. I'd never make it, and I refuse to be a hypocrite. I'm so very glad you're agreeable."

"Oh yes. Of course," she insisted. "I want to be with you, Cody. I do. I'm just not sure why you want to be with me."

"I like you. You're a good woman." He hugged her tighter. "You have a kind heart and a generous spirit. And it turns out I like freckles." He touched his lips to the end of her nose.

She grinned. He planted another smooch on her smiling mouth.

"We should go back," she told him. "We didn't behave ourselves all night in a howling blizzard only to give in now when we're going to be married in less than two weeks."

"I know. You're right." But he couldn't resist stealing one more sweet embrace before wrapping her arm around his and walking her back to town, the very image of propriety, except for the deep wrinkles crushed into the vibrant velour of her suit, her kiss-stung mouth, and his disheveled hair. He'd lost his hat some-where and never realized it.

What they looked like was a courting couple who'd been

stealing kisses. This upset a few people, but most found it reassuring. Their new pastor was no saint, just a young man, like any other young man, who happened to do his job really well. Nearly everyone felt genuinely happy for Kristina.

Cody walked his bride-to-be right back to the church so she could practice. Then he wandered over to Lydia's for an early lunch. In his contemplations, he'd completely forgotten breakfast.

Chapter Nine

One evening, a few days later, the Heitschmidts and Cody gathered again in the parlor of the family homestead. As usual, Kristina and her suitor sat rather too close together on the rose-printed sofa, their hands interlaced.

Kristina has the most beautiful hands, Cody thought, his mind turning maudlin again. He grinned at himself. *Besotted fool.*

"How are the plans coming?" James asked them, drawing Cody back to the present.

"Well," Kristina said, "on my end, I think everything is underway. I talked to Lydia about the menu for the reception, and it sounds delicious. She's keeping me in the dark about the cake, says it's her gift to us." She smiled. "The lady's altar guild has ordered me a bouquet of roses to carry, and for the rest, the silk ones in the storage room will work. I have everything I'm planning to wear ready, except the skirt Becky is making. It's almost finished. She says I can try it on tomorrow."

"As I see it," Cody added, "we have two problems. The first is music. Who is going to play for the ceremony? The best musician in town is going to be... busy."

"I mentioned it to Allison," Kristina replied. "She said we shouldn't worry. She has a plan."

Cody quirked one black eyebrow.

"I don't know what she has in mind either," Kristina replied to his unasked question, "but at this late date, there isn't much choice. We have to trust her. I'm so wrapped up in the cantata preparations, I can't even think about it until Sunday, and then it's less than a week."

Cody squeezed Kristina's hand.

Now that he'd gotten over the idea of letting a woman be in charge of the choir, things at the church were falling into place beautifully. Yesterday, Thursday, they had spent their evening together talking about the sermon, the scriptures, and the main points of the outline for Sunday's service. Kristina, upon hearing his ideas, immediately came to light with three hymns he would never have considered, but somehow fit perfectly.

How foolish I was to try to take this away from her.

He'd seen God-given gifts before, and hers was too powerful to be denied. *No wonder was angry when I tried to interfere.* Casually, gently, he'd suggested a fourth hymn for Sunday. He'd watched her go through the range of emotions from irritation to understanding to agreement. He could almost see gears turning in her head as she considered how to turn his request into something special.

The process is still ragged. We need practice working together at this, but now that we're trying to be open to each other, we're seeing success. Already, this will be a smoother service than the ones I've led up to this point.

"All right, Cody," James said, "out with it. What's the other problem?"

The question dragged him out of his contemplations. He raked his fingers through his hair. "The critical one. Who performs the ceremony? I can't marry myself."

"Oh, is that all?" James's relief showed on his face. "I'll do it."

"Can you?" Cody's eyes widened with surprise.

"Sure," James replied. "I've been head of the elder board for ten years. After the previous minister passed away, I took correspondence lessons and earned the designation of lay minister. In an emergency, I can perform weddings, baptisms and funerals as well as preach. I'm glad I don't have to do it all the time though. It isn't my calling; I was only helping out. But for my daughter..." James stopped, his eyes going distant for a moment. When he spoke again, his voice had roughened. "I think it would be fitting. And nice."

Tepid words, but the intensity of James's tone told Cody a great deal. He turned to his soon-to-be-wife and felt no surprise at seeing tears glimmering in her eyes, turning the turquoise blue more intense, like paintings he'd seen of the Mediterranean.

Cody offered a quick prayer of thanks that James had accepted him. He would be a member of the Heitschmidt family moving forward. His parents lived too far away now, both geographically and socially, for him to be more than just a visitor in their lives.

He could still remember his father's disapproval when he announced he was entering seminary, not politics. The relationship between father and son had been strained for years over the decision, but when Cody's passion for the ministry didn't wane, Harold had finally made peace with it and found him a job as associate pastor at a large and wealthy church in Austin. Unimpressed by the showy congregation, Cody had refused, preferring a poor and struggling ministry in the rough areas of Galveston. That had been the second blow to their relationship.

Only now, in occasional letters, did State Senator Harold Williams begin to show signs of respecting his son's calling.

Now I'll have a father again. Cody liked James's calm, unpretentious manner. While an important person in the town, he put on no airs and held himself superior to no one. He didn't shy from hard work and didn't hesitate to ask it of others. This was a man Cody admired and wanted to emulate.

There's only one fly in the ointment. I need advice... but I won't be getting it here.

With every passing moment, the desire grew, but he cringed to imagine the fumbling, hurried joining that was certain to follow the wedding. *I want Kristina so bad it hurts, but not like that. What to do? I suppose I'll have to ask Wesley, though I don't know if my bride's protective close friend would be much better than her father.*

"Thank you, James," Cody told his future father-in-law, forcing his thoughts back to the conversation again. "It puts my mind at ease. I guess everything is under control then."

"Oh, that reminds me," James said suddenly, "a package came for you today. Let me go get it. I'll be right back... now where did I leave that thing?"

Cody grinned as James bustled out of the room. *As if it's even possible to lose something in this immaculate house. But I'm not sorry.* James's insistence that the courting couple have a brief time of privacy each day—not enough to get into trouble, but enough to enjoy a taste of what was to come—pleased Cody tremendously.

It seemed as though every time he pulled Kristina into his arms, she transformed a bit more in his mind into the image of his ideal woman. *Or maybe that image is being transformed by her. I don't know. All I know is I want to kiss her.*

As always, she turned eagerly towards him. Whatever maidenly embarrassment she might have felt at first had long since melted in the heat of their passion. She cupped his face in long, cool fingers and drew him down, receiving the brush of his lips with a welcoming sigh. Despite his burning arousal, Cody took his time, savoring his lady's lips, memorizing this kiss, this moment, burning each touch and taste and scent into his memory.

There was no way James could have been gone for ten minutes, and neither of them heard him knock, so they were still crushed in each other's arms, tending each other's lips with passionate thoroughness, when James cleared his throat.

Kristina sprang back, her face flaming.

Cody took her hand and patted it reassuringly. Yes, they'd been caught kissing, but that was all, and James certainly hadn't been surprised. The wry look in his eyes told Cody that. He extended a parcel wrapped in brown paper, which Cody took, glancing at the return address. It came from his former advisor from the seminary.

"Well, Cody, I hate to chase you out early, but Kristina needs her rest. Tomorrow, as you might recall, is the big dress rehearsal for the cantata, and then the performance is the day after. It always wears her out, and this year it's particularly important she not get sick."

Cody nodded. In defiance of custom, he brushed his lips over Kristina's again, making her blush burn even brighter, until her cheeks outshone her hair, and then he squeezed her hand gently and left.

Outside, the night temperature had dropped to a frigid low. It appeared the weather was turning back towards winter again.

As he made his way through the clear, frosty night, his mind played over the next few days. Tomorrow, along with putting the finishing touches on his sermon, he'd be at choir practice for three hours in the afternoon.

Sunday would also be busier than usual with a regular service in the morning and the cantata in the evening. During the week, Kristina needed to evaluate what furniture she would require to make the vicarage livable for a lady with high standards. Tuesday, his parents were due to arrive. Despite what was sure to be wild last-minute preparations, choir practice was taking place on Wednesday as usual. Christmas would not be postponed. The wedding would be Friday afternoon, and he had a Christmas Eve service *and* another Sunday to prepare for immediately afterward.

What a flurry. James was absolutely right to send me on my way and make Kristina rest.

With so much on his mind, Cody found himself at his front door sooner than he expected. His thoughts still far away, he absently let himself into the vicarage, flung his coat on the arm of the sofa and dropped the package on the seat. The fire was dying, so he poked at it with an iron utensil and added a couple of logs.

Then, as light and heat flared in the room, he untied the coarse twine holding shut the paper wrapping and looked inside. A book, simply bound in stiffened gray paper with black lettering, bore the name *A Christian Man's Guide to Marriage* by George Wilson. Cody had never heard of an author by that name. He opened the cover and found a note from his former mentor inside.

Dear Cody,

Congratulations on your upcoming marriage. Unfortunately, I will not be able to attend, as the event is so close to Christmas, but I wanted to send a gift. Based on the conversations we've had, I think this book might be useful to you. Read it right away. Best wishes.

Dr. Abraham Thomas

Cody grinned. He'd learned so much from Dr. Thomas, and his note, like his conversation style and sermons, was succinct, blunt, and straightforward. "The gospel is simple, son," he'd told him, "and most folks like that simplicity. Unless you're planning to preach in your daddy's fancy church for politicians, bring the people the message and don't put on airs. They'll thank you for it."

It had been good advice, and Cody had kept it to this day.

And now here's some new advice: read this book right away. I don't have much time for reading, but I'd hate to ignore Dr. Thomas.

Opening to the introduction, Cody's face went slack with shock. This was not a book about being kind to your wife or listening to her opinions.

The first line he read nearly jumped off the page and slapped him on the head.

Congratulations, young man, on keeping yourself chaste in preparation for your upcoming marriage. You may be wondering how to proceed and hoping it will all work out. You may also be wondering what the scriptures have to say on the subject of marital intimacy.

This book addresses these questions from a Biblical and medical perspective. After reading, you should be able to engage in the God-given act of intimacy with confidence you and your wife will both find the process uplifting and enjoyable.

Before you begin, here is some strong advice, to be ignored at your peril. Do not begin reading this more than two weeks before your wedding. It contains strongly-worded information which you will likely find arousing. Reading too far ahead is not wise.

Next, under no circumstances should you be alone with your bride once you begin. No doubt your control is already tenuous. You didn't wait this long to miss the prize at the end...

Cody considered the book, leafing through the pages and scanning the illustrations with interest. *Well, there are less than two weeks until the wedding, and I'll scarcely have a moment alone with Kristina between now and then, so all should be well.*

Cody set the book down and crossed the room to the wash-basin, where he cleaned his teeth before stripping down to his undergarments, wrapping himself in a blanket, and settling back to read.

Chapter Ten

D ecember 15th, cantata night, began illuminated by a sunset that hung long and low over the horizon, staining the sky the exact golden red of Kristina's hair. Cody could still feel the soft strands of her burnished mane sliding through his fingers.

Five days until the wedding, and he felt properly enamored. His brain, muddled to mush by the thoughts of his entrancing bride, kept spewing out the most maudlin thoughts at random moments, distracting him from everyday life. This usually earned him a knowing smirk from whoever happened to catch him daydreaming.

The distraction was growing worse too, with every passing day. This morning the sermon had been somewhat less than stellar, and his eyes refused to stay on his notes, drawn continuously as they were to the balcony.

In the end, he'd managed to stumble his way through, and then he'd spent the rest of the afternoon reading. This activity turned his mind even more towards Kristina, imagining her in all the various positions the book described.

Five days. We'll be married Friday afternoon.

His eyes scanned the horizon again. The prairie really did

resemble the ocean. It lay as far as the eye could see in any direction, the surface rippling gently in the wind. Though the Rocky Mountains lay only a short distance to the west, they were invisible from here. Not even a hill, hardly a tree altered the landscape. Only mile after unchanging mile of swaying grass.

"Lord," Cody said aloud from his spot on the church step, where he leaned against the wrought-iron railing. His breath misted in the cold December air. "I believe this is your will. I believe you've given me Kristina. She's just what I've always wanted and needed in a wife. Help me, Lord, to give her all she wants and needs as well. Help me love her."

He looked over the horizon again. Red faded to orange, then to gold. Above, blue built upon blue until it grew nearly night-dark overhead. Just below the twilight band stretched a stripe the color of her eyes.

Cody smiled. His gaze returned to earth, to the freckled face of his angel. Kristina approached the church, a sheaf of sheet music clutched to her chest. She wore a coat in a cheerful shade of crimson, cut close to her curves. Below that, a chocolate-colored skirt billowed in the wind. Hats turned out to be all but hopeless here, and her hair was escaping from its pins bit by bit.

She greeted him with one of her brilliant smiles. Cody grabbed her arms and kissed her, in full view of the street, not caring what anyone thought.

She stiffened in surprise, a squeak escaping her, but then, as always, she acquiesced to his demand, letting herself have another little taste of her man. Then she pulled away and hurried inside.

He pursued her with long-legged strides inside the door and up the staircase to the balcony. He watched while she set music on each hard, wooden chair. The last and biggest stack went to the music stand above the keyboard of the organ.

When her arms were finally empty, he reached for her again.

"Cody," she said firmly, laying a hand on his chest, "stop this. The choir will be here any minute to warm up. Let's not be silly."

She's right. I know she is. But his arms ached to hold her.

He gave her a sad-eyed gaze. "One kiss, darlin'? Just a little one?"

She giggled. "Cody, I don't think you remember how to give little kisses anymore."

"Maybe not," he said, "but it's your fault. If you weren't so sweet..." While she was distracted by blushing over the compliment, he grabbed her and planted a big wet smooch on her lips. Then he obediently trailed to the back of the choir area and took his seat in the bass section, scooping up his music and schooling his face into an expression of intense innocence, just as the first choir members arrived for the warmup.

Allison and Becky took one look at Cody's fake smile and Kristina's pinkened lips and burst out laughing.

The ladies took their seats. Allison on the alto side, Becky with the sopranos. More choir members arrived, making their way up to their seats near the organ while a pair of young matrons herded the children into the sanctuary and then headed to the front to raid the store room.

Kristina blushed as the long, white angel dress emerged and was handed to thirteen-year-old Prudence Walker. The tall young lady had hair two shades redder than Kristina's, but only a few pretty freckles across her nose and cheeks.

Turning her attention back to the choir, Kristina blinked to realize almost everyone had arrived while she daydreamed. Only one empty seat remained in the bass section. *Wesley. Poor man. We'll have to start without him; there's no time to wait.* He and Melissa, who was playing a sheep, would either make it, or they wouldn't.

Kristina seated herself on the bench, not of the organ, but of the small upright piano beside it. Playing a fast series of scales to loosen up her fingers, she turned to the choir. Then she struck a major chord.

"All right everyone," she said, and the murmured conversation instantly died. "With me. La-la-la-la-la." Kristina sang the usual five-note descending scale, and the choir instantly joined her. After scales, they moved on to a couple of other warm-ups before touching on a few of the trickiest pieces in the music.

"Well now," she told them as she wrapped up the melody check, "everything sounds marvelous, this is going to be great. Do what you just did, and this will be the best Christmas cantata ever."

"Children?" she called down over the balcony. Little faces looked up. "Your turn." She played the simple opening to 'Away in a Manger', and the children began to sing, a charming mixture of angelic and off-key that would make the mothers weep.

As she played the accompaniment, a sudden image crossed Kristina's mind, of a red-haired little girl with blue eyes, standing among the children, singing. *My daughter. Mine and Cody's.* Her fingers began to tremble. *That could happen, it is possible.* She tried to picture herself as a mother and promptly hit a shocking wrong note.

The children's choir screeched to a halt, and the adults stared.

"Oops," she said, as her cheeks burned. "Sorry, everyone. That sounds great, children, I think we're all set. Why don't you get in your places? We'll start in about ten minutes."

The mothers herded the children to their reserved seats in the back two rows of the church. Kristina could hear them telling a quiet story to keep the little ones entertained and out of mischief while they waited for the service to begin. It was a few minutes too early to begin the prelude, so the choir turned to each other and began murmuring in low voices.

Cody rose, approached his betrothed, and took her hand. He didn't kiss it, only gave a gentle squeeze, but his eyes held the same burning heat that had alarmed her earlier.

"Cody," she told him in an almost inaudible undertone, "you have to concentrate on church now."

He quirked an eyebrow at her.

"I know. I feel it too. Come on, Pastor, concentrate. Christmas isn't going to wait for us."

He smiled, squeezed her hand again, and headed down to greet the people who were beginning to arrive.

There was a squeak of a tiny voice and then a clatter on the stairs as Wesley finally turned up. He shot the director a contrite look. She nodded to him, and he went to take his seat, second from the end, leaving room for Cody to slip in and sing, and then sneak out again to give the message.

Five minutes to seven. Kristina moved to the organ bench and began playing prelude music, the Pastoral Symphony from Handel's *Messiah.*

The congregation began to arrive. They'd been asked to enter the church quietly this evening so they could contemplate the solemnity of the occasion. They appeared mostly to be honoring the request. There was a low hum of conversation from a few people, but mostly just the swishing of skirts and trousers and the soft thump of boots on the wooden planks of the floor.

The appointed hour arrived. A loud clunk indicated the outside door had been closed. A soft step on the stairs and Kristina watched her handsome pastor slip across the balcony and slide into his seat beside Wesley. The two men shook hands and Kristina played a single note on the piano, softly, before rising to stand in front of them. She indicated for the choir to stand, and lifted her arms. They inhaled as one and sang their opening anthem, in its sad minor key, all in unison.

Let all mortal flesh keep silence,
And with fear and trembling stand;
Ponder nothing earthly minded,
For with blessing in His hand,
Christ our God to earth descendeth
Our full homage to demand.

At His feet the six-winged seraph,
Cherubim with sleepless eye,
Veil their faces to the presence,
As with ceaseless voice they cry:
Alleluia, Alleluia
Alleluia, Lord Most High!

A closing motion of her hand brought the lingering final note to a stop, and she waved them to their seats.

Cody moved to the front of the balcony and said, "Let us pray. Oh Lord, we gather together tonight in honor of your birth. May the songs of our lips and the meditations of our hearts bring honor and glory to You. Amen."

Several members of the congregation repeated the amen.

Another, softer voice spoke from the front of the room. Alan Fulton, one of Wesley's many cousins, stood to one side of the communion rail and read the first scripture.

Thus, the Christmas cantata began. Kristina had created it to be a blend of choir anthems and hymns, scriptures and skits. It was far from perfect, as one would expect from a production involving children. The Angel of the Lord spoke so softly, Kristina felt sure the elderly parishioners in the back row couldn't hear a word. One of the kings tripped over his robe and went sprawling, flattening his box of 'gold'. Mary forgot her lines.

On the positive side, the choir sounded wonderful. The music Cody had complained was too hard went off without a hitch, even the complicated 'Glory to God' from *The Messiah*. As one of the difficult polyphonic sections rolled along, Cody caught her eye and winked. She beamed at him.

Below, Alan read the final scripture. "In the beginning was the Word, and the Word was with God, and the Word was God. The same was in the beginning with God. All things were made by him; and without him was not anything made that was made. In him was life; and the life was the light of men. And the light shineth in darkness; and the darkness comprehended it not.

"He was in the world, and the world was made by him, and the world knew him not. He came unto his own, and his own received him not. But as many as received him, to them gave the power to become the sons of God, even to them that believe on his name: Which were born, not of blood, nor of the will of the flesh, nor of the will of man, but of God. And the Word was made flesh, and dwelt among us, and we beheld his glory, the glory as of the only begotten of the Father, full of grace and truth."

While Alan read, Prudence lit a candle from the one on the pulpit and moved among the congregation. Each person had taken a candle upon entering the room, and they received the light, passing it down the rows until the sanctuary was lit with dozens of tiny sparks.

Kristina played a soft note on the piano and the choir began to sing, *a cappella*. In honor of so many members, they sang the first verse in German. Then they switched to English and the congregation joined in. "Silent night, holy night. All is calm. All is bright..."

The soft song ended, and the congregation began to file out, keeping their candles to light their way. At last, only the pastor and the musician remained. They extinguished the lamps on the balcony and descended the stairs hand in hand to put out the lights below. In silence, they moved to the back of the darkened church, where Cody tenderly wrapped Kristina in her coat, buttoning the front for her before shrugging on his winter garments.

Then he took her hand and walked her through the dark and silent streets, illuminated by the full moon sparkling on a fall of fresh snow. For once, no wind blew. The night seemed to be holding its breath. All was clear and cold and clean.

They arrived at Kristina's home all too soon, but this time, when Cody pulled his bride-to-be into his arms and lowered his mouth to hers, she offered no protest. They clung, emotions overwhelmed by the nostalgia of the service, pouring out powerful, unnamed feelings in a kiss that defied description.

Long they stood, cradling each other in the moonlight, trying desperately to say with their touches what words could never express. And then, of his own will, Cody released Kristina and brushed his thumb over her lower lip.

"Good night, darlin'," he breathed softly, mere inches from her face.

"Good night," she replied. They kissed once more, a soft, swift brush of lips, and then Kristina turned and stepped inside.

Up in her room, Kristina changed into her nightgown and cleaned her teeth. She felt close to tears.

This will be my last Christmas cantata as a single woman. This time next year, I'll be long married, but I'll never forget this night. It was perfect. Cody was part of that perfection, and so was I. It was a heady, novel experience, and one she was fiercely glad not to have missed.

She stretched out in the bed, shivering on the icy sheets as she waited for her body heat to warm them so she could sleep. A strong sensation of warm arms holding her suffused her body. Wrapped in the imagined embrace of her beloved, sweet thoughts blended into lovely dreams.

Chapter Eleven

O n Monday at noon, Kristina struggled to keep her mind busy and her nerves at bay while she and Cody stood near the train station, awaiting the arrival of Cody's parents.

After another brief warming trend, the day had turned bitingly cold, and little puffs of frozen breath emanated from them and from the other people assembled to await the arrivals.

Kristina's hand trembled on Cody's arm, and she felt sure it was not entirely from the chill. He patted her reassuringly. She gave him a worried glance and then turned to look at the scenery.

Well, such scenery as it is. The train station—located at the southernmost part of town—consisted of little more than an open-sided, barn-like structure with a red roof and four stout pillars to hold it up, which provided minimal shelter for those disembarking in harsh weather.

Across the tracks, a single worker sat shivering in a minuscule booth just large enough for his chair and a built-in shelf on which his cash box and pricing chart rested.

They'll be here any minute, and then what? Nerves churned in Kristina's belly. To keep her attention diverted from her nausea, she reflected on the progress they'd been making over the last week.

I moved into Dad's guest room so the bed could go to the vicarage. Then the wardrobe. There was no way that flimsy rack and its ragged curtain would work for me. But goodness, wasn't it strange—and far too real—to see Cody's suits hanging next to my dresses?

She'd added a few simple decorations to the house as well. A painting of Jesus praying in the garden hung above the sofa in the parlor area. Another of an old man praying in front of a bowl of soup and a loaf of bread graced the wall behind the dining table.

Another memory brought a faint smile to her lips. *Dad wanted to send his cuckoo clock. I think he's tired of the noisy contraption, but in that wide-open room, it would keep us awake all night. Sorry, dad, you'll have to keep on contending with the obnoxious little bird on your own.*

Her attention shifted from the past to the present. Beyond the station, the level ground stretched away to the horizon. The frozen prairie grass swayed stiffly in the wind, and occasionally a stalk snapped under the strain to fall, limp and sad as a slain soldier, against the remains of its comrades. To the left and right, the same scene repeated, mile after mile, until the curve of the earth rendered the miles invisible. In all three directions, only the occasional farmhouse or stunted tree—twisted by the endless wind—interrupted the endless prairie.

Only behind them, to the north, was life and color, the thriving little community on the edge of the endless grasslands. Suddenly, Kristina felt small and insignificant. *Against the eternal persistence of nature, what is one person, one town? The prairie has always been, and no matter how much we build, there will come a day when we're gone, and the prairie will take over again, blotting out the remains of our endeavors.*

"'Only one life. Twill soon be past. Only what's done for Christ will last,'" Cody quoted.

Kristina's fingers slipped between his. *The way with think alike can be a bit overwhelming... but nice.*

Far off in the distance, a whistle blared.

In a landscape so open, the flash of the sun reflecting off the train became visible a long while before the puffing black beast neared the station, a plume of smoke floating off into the sky. The closer it came, the more Kristina's fingers tightened on Cody's, until he grimaced and patted her hand. She relaxed her grip, blushing beyond the color painted on her cheeks by the frigid wind.

As the engine chugged beneath the station roof and pulled through, allowing the passenger cars to unload under the shelter, Cody touched his lips to Kristina's cheek. This earned them a disapproving snort from one elderly woman, who nailed them with an angry glare and leaned forward threateningly on the silver-headed cane that groaned under her weight.

Cody shot her a disarming grin, and her expression softened.

A long, loud screech of steam escaping from the smokestack signaled the end of the journey, and the porters opened the doors, helping long-skirted ladies and gentlemen in suits to disembark from the passenger car. The December wind immediately sent several hats flying away across the prairie, never to be seen again.

Kristina grinned.

A handsome couple of middle years climbed uncomfortably down the stairs. The gentleman wore a suit in a distinguished shade of deep brown. His black hair—silvered at the temples—was combed and slicked with pomade. A thick, luxurious mustache adorned his upper lip. A lovely woman hung on his arm. Her blond hair was fading to silver, but her figure remained trim. She wore a maroon bustled skirt and matching jacket over a gleaming white shirtwaist, fastened with an expensive-looking cameo at the throat.

Upon reaching the ground, she scanned the crowd with brilliant blue eyes until she spotted Cody. Then a wide smile broke over her face, crinkling the skin around her eyes and mouth. She dropped her husband's arm and ran to her son, throwing herself into his arms. He released Kristina's hand and crushed his mother in a hug.

"Oh, love, look at you!" she said in a soft drawl. She kissed his cheek loudly.

Kristina smiled at the woman's exuberance. *Cody's mother adores him, a sentiment I completely understand.*

"It's good to see you too, Mama. You look as beautiful as ever."

Mrs. Williams brushed aside the compliment with a laugh, but Kristina agreed with her fiancé's assessment.

Footsteps crunched on the gravel and Kristina looked up to meet the steel-gray eyes of the man who could only be Cody's father. *So, this is where he got most of his looks.* But whereas an appealing grin softened Cody's handsome face and muscular figure to friendliness, his father was stern-faced and uncomfortably rigid in his stance.

She wanted to slink away from him and hide. But of course, her stubborn nature would allow no such thing. Straightening her spine—wishing she'd worn her seldom-used corset to restrain that extra two inches of waist—she extended her hand and plastered what she hoped was a confident smile on her face. "You must be Senator Williams," she said. "I'm glad to meet you. Cody has told me so much about you."

The senator winced visibly at her casual use of his son's Christian name.

Are people really so formal in Austin as to expect a woman on the verge of marriage to call her intended by his title? If so, too bad. I won't do it.

"I wish he'd told us something about you," the man replied, "but there's nothing to be done about it now. Harold Williams." He took her hand with an air of frustrated longsuffering and gave her a halfhearted pat with his free hand.

"Kristina Heitschmidt," she replied, forcing a courteous salutation.

He pumped her hand once and dropped her.

"I'm delighted to meet you, Miss Heitschmidt." Cody's mother had released her stranglehold on her son, shot her husband a warning glance, and clasped both of Kristina's hands eagerly in hers.

"Kristina, please, ma'am," she insisted. "We're nearly family, after all."

"That we are, Kristina," Cody's mother replied with a smile as big and sunny as a Kansas sunflower, "and you must call me Marguerite."

Kristina grinned, a genuine smile this time.

"Now let me take a look at you, my dear."

Kristin's smile turned wooden. She had taken extra pains with her appearance that morning, puffing her strawberry blond hair at the crown before pinning it into a complicated braided bun. Her green wool skirt contrasted cheerfully with her long red coat. She wore her black boots again. Though uncomfortable, she didn't want to risk her gray ones in the dirty slush that gathered in the low points of the street. Overall, she looked prim and proper... except for her face. Those impossible freckles would never allow her to look distinguished the way this lovely woman did.

Kristina regarded Cody's mother in a silent frenzy of nerves. And then another broad smile broke over the woman's face. "Well, aren't you just cute as a bug," she drawled, her tone utterly sincere. "No wonder Cody likes you."

She sounds... charmed. Astonished, Kristina's hands dropped to her sides. *Mrs. Williams thinks I'm cute? She approves Cody's choice?* This was far more than Kristina had expected, and tears stung her eyes. "Thank you, ma'am," she said in an unsteady voice.

"Hello, son," Harold said, in his restrained, chilly tone.

"Father." Cody's voice matched his father's.

"So, this is the goal to which you're putting all that education?" Harold turned his eyes to the tiny town on the edge of the prairie, took it in, and dismissed it as nothing, all in the space of a single heartbeat.

"Yes, Father. It is. I love it here." He reached out and took Kristina's hand in his.

"Very well then. I, for one, am famished. Is there anywhere to eat in this...?" he trailed off and waved his hand toward Garden City.

"Oh, yes, sir. Of course," Kristina jumped in, defending her home. "Lydia's Café is just up the street. She serves wonderful lunches."

"Can't you summon a cab? It's cold out here."

"Um, no. Sorry. There are no cabs in Garden City."

Howard looked askance at her. "How do you people get around?"

"We walk," she replied. "There's nothing too far to reach on foot."

Harold muttered inarticulately under his breath.

I'm just as glad I don't know what he said.

He continued grumbling as they walked up the slushy, muddy street, glaring at his shiny black shoes as though daring the mud to stain the gleaming surface. On his arm, his wife chattered cheerfully with Cody about people he knew back in Austin and what they were doing now. He appeared to be listening politely but not with a great deal of attention. His fingers stroked Kristina's hand where it rested on his bicep. The gentle caress reminded her this was Tuesday afternoon.

Three days. Suddenly her lungs felt too tight and a thrill of nauseous excitement shot through her belly. Every evening the attention Cody paid her increased in heat and intensity. He had ignited a fire in her that only he could quench. *Three days.*

She shook off the inappropriate thought and tried to focus on the conversation. It was not particularly interesting, as she knew none of the people in question, but she attended to it nonetheless. It gave her nervous mind something to do, rather than obsessing about what was to come.

At last, the wooden shingle appeared, announcing they had arrived at their destination. Kristina entered first, so she wouldn't have to look at Harold's expression as when he saw the little café with its warped floorboards, uneven tables and mismatched chairs.

The shabbiness of this place is part of its charm. My opinion isn't going to be altered because some snooty Texas politician looks down his nose at it.

The four took a seat around a battered pine table. A moment later Lydia stopped by, greeting her friends with a cheerful, round-cheeked smile.

"Soup and sandwiches today, everyone," she said by way of greeting. "And would you like coffee, tea, or buttermilk?"

"Coffee, please," Kristina said.

"That sounds good," Cody agreed.

"Indeed, it does," Harold added.

"I'd prefer a cup of tea," Marguerite requested.

"Coming right up." Lydia bustled away, returning with a huge tray laden with food and drinks, which she distributed to the family.

Kristina lifted her cup. The hot beverage warmed her insides even as the heat belching from the industrial oven in the next room thawed her frozen fingers and nose. A delicious waft of chicken and vegetables elicited an indiscreet growl from her stomach.

They sipped and munched in contented silence for a time before Marguerite spoke again. "What do you like to do, my dear?" she asked Kristina.

"Kristina's a musician," Cody replied between bites.

"A musician?" Harold at last showed a glimmer of approval. His gaze turned to Kristina, but as her mouth was full of sandwich, she indicated Cody with a tilt of the head.

"Yes," Cody told his father, taking up the reigns of the conversation. "She plays the organ and the piano at the church. She directs the choir too."

"Oh," said Harold, his interest deflating, "a church musician. Of course."

"No, not at all," Cody protested. "She's the church musician now, and we're blessed to have her, but she could just as easily be a concert organist. She's trained for it."

"Are you?" Harold turned to Kristina in astonishment.

She swallowed her bite of sandwich. "Almost," she replied with brutal honesty. "I attended a conservatory in Kansas City for three years, but I stopped short of completing the course of study."

"Why?" He looked like a storm cloud now.

"My mother died," was all Kristina said. *How I miss her! On the verge of marriage, there are so many questions I want to ask, so many things I need to know, but she's gone.*

She closed her eyes against the sudden sting, and when she opened them and pasted an overly bright expression on her face again, she felt like an utter fraud. *False smile. False musician.* But the affection she felt for Cody was real. If that counted for anything with his parents, it was a start.

She looked up from her bowl.

Harold met her eyes, the steel gaze softening to silver. "I'm sorry," he told her, and the arrogance had drained from his voice.

They regarded each other in silence, and then he gave a slight, almost imperceptible nod and returned his attention to his dinner. She had no idea how to interpret his gesture.

Silence fell across the table for a few more minutes, and then Marguerite piped up again. "Cody never could be bothered with all the feminine fripperies, but I'm dying to know. What are the plans for the wedding?"

She's good at fixing lulls in the conversation, Kristina thought, allowing herself to be drawn out of her contemplative mood. "It all came together a bit fast, but what we have in mind is pretty simple, so that works."

"I can understand that," Marguerite replied. "When you love your fiancé so much, you just want to hurry up and get it done."

That feels right, though we haven't said the words yet. Kristina glanced at Cody and saw him devouring her with his eyes. She colored.

"What will you wear? There was no time for a fancy dress, I suppose."

"No, but my best friend's sister is a seamstress, so she's making me a fancy white skirt. It should go well with my favorite white blouse..."

"All white!" Marguerite crowed. "Oh, that's lovely. White weddings are all the rage. I can't wait to tell my friends that my son had one too! They'll be so jealous." She beamed.

Her exuberance relieved a great deal of Kristina's nerves. *Well, nerves about my future in-laws, anyway. Nerves about the wedding will be my constant companions until it's done.*

At last, the meal ended, and Cody and his fiancée walked his parents to the hotel so they could wash up and rest. At the door, Marguerite enfolded Kristina in a friendly hug.

"Would you two like to come to dinner at my house this evening?" Kristina asked.

Harold gave her another one of those stormy glares. "Without Cody?"

This time she laughed. "No, with Cody, of course. He eats with us every night now. I didn't think to invite him because I assumed he would be there."

"I'll be there," Cody confirmed, squeezing the hand that was, once again, clutched tightly in his. Then he turned to his parents. "I'll stop by the hotel around six and take y'all over, all right?"

"Sure, son. That sounds fine," Harold replied, looking up at the five-story rectangle of red bricks, with a hint of that judgmental attitude returning to his expression. "Occidental Hotel?"

"Yes," Kristina replied. "It's a good place to sleep, but I don't recommend eating in the restaurant."

"There's a restaurant?" Harold asked. "A real one, with menus?"

"Yes," Kristina said, "but you should know the nickname of this place is the Accidental Hotel because if you ever get anything to eat, it would be by accident."

Harold tried to suppress his chuckle. He failed. This time, when he took Kristina's hand, he shook it warmly. Then he and his wife headed inside while Cody slipped his arm around Kristina's waist and escorted her home.

Up in their room on the third floor, Marguerite set her shoulder bag down on a small, round table with an unimpressive maple finish. The bed, though rather narrow for two, sported a handsome head and footboard of brass, and when she sat down on the mattress, she discovered it was also comfortable. *This red and blue crazy quilt isn't much to my taste, but it looks warm, and goodness knows, we'll need that come evening.*

"Harold," she spoke, capturing his attention away from his task of hanging clothing in the wardrobe.

"What?"

"What were you doing today?"

"What do you mean?" he asked, turning to face her.

She met his eyes squarely and gave him a look she'd taught him to dread over the years of their marriage. "Why were you so unkind to Kristina?"

"Unkind? No, I was surprised. I can't believe our son is marrying such a homely woman."

The disapproving look sharpened as Marguerite let Harold know he was in deep trouble.

"She's not homely in the slightest," she insisted, in a tone that chilled the room faster than the drafts seeping in around the windows. "She's adorable. And so sweet and friendly. I think she and Cody are a great match. You can see how much they care about each other. Admit it, Harold. He's never *ever* looked at a girl in such a way before."

"He hasn't."

"And he's an adult, capable of making his own decisions. I'm pleased he went for a woman of character rather than just a pretty face."

"I know he makes his own decisions," Harold grumbled. "He stopped listening to me when he was sixteen."

Marguerite bounced up off the bed and went to her husband, wrapping her arms around him to soften the blow of what she was about to say. "That's because you were trying to steer him into a life for which he wasn't suited, and which he didn't want. I think, after all this time, you have to agree he was right."

"Yes," her husband said, "I see that." And his voice did not sound grumpy anymore. There was an odd note in his tone.

"Why, Harold," Marguerite cooed, "are you... proud of your son?"

"Yes. Why wouldn't I be? He paid his own way through seminary, never taking a penny from me, refused the position I found for him, and now he's a respected member of a community, albeit a small and humble one. So, yes, I'm proud of him. He's proven himself. And I won't have to worry about any scandals like some of my colleagues have faced with their sons."

"Well, sugar," Marguerite replied, "don't you think it's about time you told *him*? I know Cody would like your approval... of his career and his wife."

"I know. I will. I just wanted to see if he would pursue his goals *without* my approval. Now I know he can and will succeed on his own, and he's his own man, I'll give him my approval. I still don't understand Miss Heitschmidt though."

His wife tickled him. In public, she would never have dared, but in their private moments, she kept firm control of her husband, using this magic technique to shocking advantage. Reduced to helpless laughter, unable to break free from the grip of her delicate fingers, he at last turned and distracted her with a long kiss before scooping her up in his arms.

"I think," he said, depositing her on the bed, "we're supposed to be resting." Then he kicked off his shoes and climbed on beside her.

Chapter Twelve

riday. It's Friday. Kristina's eyes shot open, and she groaned. The winter sunlight felt painfully bright. She'd tossed and turned in nervous excitement until well after midnight. *Now it's my wedding day, and I don't want to get out of bed.* Well, perhaps *she* did, but her body did not.

Thump! Thump! Thump! "Princess, you need to get up."

"Ugh," Kristina groaned in response, throwing her arm over her face.

"I know, honey, but Allison and Rebecca are already here. It's ten o'clock."

"Ten? Oh no!" Kristina hoisted herself from the bed and stumbled over to the washstand to splash water on her face.

"Are you up?"

"Yes, Dad. I'm up."

"Do you want any breakfast?"

"No thank you." Kristina's stomach churned so badly she couldn't bear the thought of food. "But if there's any coffee left..."

"I just made a fresh pot for the girls," he replied, "I'll have them bring you a cup."

"Bless you, Dad," she replied. Then she quickly washed up and donned fresh undergarments. She was brushing the knots from her long red hair when her friends walked in. Becky had a bundle of fabric in her arms, Allison carefully balanced three cups of coffee in hers. She set them on a piece of loose sheet music, which Kristina had uncharacteristically abandoned on her dressing table, and went to envelop her friend in a tight hug.

"I'm so happy for you, darling," she whimpered, tears pooling in the corners of her eyes.

"Don't you dare," Kristina scolded. "You never cry. If you start now, you'll set me off, and I'll never be able to stop."

"Okay," Allison said, and then turned away to hide her brimming eyes.

"Should I get dressed?" Kristina asked. "I know you said the skirt might need a last-minute adjustment."

"Nope," Becky replied. "I won't have you drinking coffee in a white skirt. Don't dress until you know you won't be doing anything... staining."

To distract herself from her churning stomach, Kristina regarded the two sisters. It never ceased to amaze her that siblings could look so utterly different. Allison, tall, curvy, and athletic, had a full, lush figure and a gorgeous face with deep dimples in both cheeks.

Becky was tiny, petite and slender, with quick nimble fingers and restrained, lovely features. Her soft hazel eyes crinkled a bit as she smiled at Kristina.

A long string of miscarriages meant more than a decade separated the sisters. Becky, though well over thirty and single, was a loving and loyal friend, possessed of a quiet grace Kristina had used as a model to curb the excesses of her turbulent adolescence.

She gave the younger sister a quick hug, and let Becky press her into a high-backed, lacquered chair with an embroidered cushion, which Allison had placed in front of the mirror. Kristina retrieved her cup and sipped the dark brew gratefully as Allison continued running the brush through her hair.

"Do you want anything in particular?" she asked, playing with the ends and making Kristina shiver. *Or maybe it's the cold.* The window admitted a bit of wintry air and she was dressed only in her unmentionables.

"I have no idea," Kristina replied. "I can't even think straight, I'm so excited and nervous."

"You sound like a bride," Becky commented, gulping the last of her coffee and pulling the skirt out of its wrapping. From the corner of her eye, Kristina could see the fabric shimmering in the sunlight. She swallowed hard, determined not to cry.

"Now then," Allison quipped, continuing to brush her friend's hair, "you're embarking on one of life's great adventures. Is there anything you need to know about... what happens next?"

"Yes, but I think I'm out of luck," Kristina replied tartly, "neither of you knows any more than I do."

All three ladies began to laugh, Kristina rather hysterically. And then abruptly the giggles turned to sobs. Becky retrieved the mostly empty coffee cup before her friend could slosh its remaining contents on her bloomers. Allison dropped the brush and hugged her from behind.

"What is it, Kristina?" Allison asked. "Nerves?"

"Yes, partly," she sniffled in reply.

"What else then?"

"I miss Mom. She should be here with me, giving me an embarrassing lecture about my 'wifely duties'. Calvin should be here. Half my family is gone."

"I know, honey. It's so hard." Allison's hug tightened further.

"And..." Kristina broke off.

"What?" Allison wanted to know

"Well, just look at me. What do I have to offer a handsome, desirable man like Cody?"

Becky shook her head. "Don't be foolish, Kristina. You have a lot to offer him. And you're not ugly either."

"But I'm not beautiful. Not even pretty."

"Your spirit is beautiful," Allison told her. "Cody can see it, that's why he wants you. No one really believed you two misbehaved. You could have gotten away with not marrying. We all just assumed you wanted to and were using the potential scandal as an excuse to hurry it along. Be honest, Kristina. Isn't that what happened?"

She lifted her tear-stained face and looked from one friend to the other. "I suppose so."

"And he's right there with you, pushing the fast pace. He wants to be married to you, Kristina," added Becky, who pulled a handkerchief from the bureau drawer and handed it to her friend. "Now, don't worry about those tears," she continued. "Brides cry. I see it all the time. You'll be fine, and you'll still be married whether you cry or not." She squeezed Kristina's shoulder and went back to the bed, smoothing out the satin and making sure not even a hint of a wrinkle marred the icy fabric.

"You'd better eat something," Allison told her. "It's three hours until the wedding. You don't want to faint, do you?"

"Of course not, but I'm afraid I'll be sick."

"You won't. You'll probably feel better. Becky, can you go get her something? I have an idea about this hair. Kristina, where are your hairpins?"

"In the bureau."

As Becky left the room, Allison crossed to the bureau and retrieved several racks of hairpins.

By the time the first section of Kristina's hair had been shaped into a loose sweep that curved across the back of her head and wrapped around itself to form the start of a knot, Becky had returned with a plate of buttered bread.

Kristina regarded the repast warily but took a bite. She quickly discovered her friends were right, and she did feel better for eating. The bread settled her churning stomach and it also took her mind off the pins digging into her sensitive scalp.

When the bread was gone and her coiffure completed, Kristina washed her hands and Becky finally allowed her to dress. She pulled out her fanciest shirtwaist, the one with vertical pleats along the entire front, each one covered in a fragment of lace. Buttoning the garment up to her throat, she added the rose enamel brooch. Then Becky carefully opened the skirt, so she could step in. The front, like the shirtwaist, gathered in a series of pleats at Kristina's slender waistline. Just past her knees, the pleats ended in a row of pink satin roses, below which the fabric fell loose to the floor. The back of the skirt consisted of two layers, one on top of the other, edged in pink satin ribbon.

Kristina studied herself in the mirror. Tears threatened again, but she swallowed them down. Allison lifted the veil of thin lace, with its row of white flowers, and pinned it to her hair.

Now I look like a bride. A single tear escaped and flowed down her cheek. She dabbed at it with her handkerchief before stuffing the little scrap of fabric inside her sleeve.

They had been at work by this time for almost two hours. The cuckoo downstairs announced that noon had arrived, and the wedding was due to start at one. The Ladies' Altar Guild should already be at the church adding a few white flowers to the Christmas decorations, so there was nothing left to do but wait.

James knocked on the door again, and this time Becky admitted him into the room. He cut quite a dashing figure in his long-tailed black suit, his hair neatly combed, and the spinster's eyes seemed to linger on him. He took one look at his daughter and froze. Kristina turned and raced into his arms, all attempts at restraint abandoned.

Inside the vicarage, Cody paced the room nervously, dressed in the black trousers and white shirt his father had brought from Austin but lacking his collar, tie, and coat.

"Where is she?" he growled.

"She'll be back any minute," Harold reassured his son. "There's an hour left before the ceremony, and it's not like they'll start it without you."

"I can't believe she forgot it."

"Cody, settle down. She said she was sorry. She'll be back with the ring any minute. Now please finish getting dressed. Do you want any help with your tie?"

Cody was still glowering and muttering when his father finished affixing his cufflinks.

"You make quite the bridegroom, son," Howard told him. "You certainly surprised me with your telegram. What made you decide to do this, and so quickly?"

"I wanted to. Kristina is... very special. I would be a fool to let her go, and I'm not a fool."

"I suppose not. Well, thus far your judgment has proven excellent, so I'll have to take your word for it this woman is all you say."

"She's wonderful, Father, I'm blessed to have her. Where is Mother?" Cody flung himself down on the sofa. The door creaked as Marguerite slipped in, clutching a little object in her hand.

"Here you go, son," she said, "and with plenty of time to spare."

Cody snatched the ring from her hand and said nothing as he turned it over in his palm, admiring the large white moonstone in a delicate filigree setting. It had adorned his grandmother's finger for as long as he could remember, and now it would be for his wife. *Wife. Kristina.* He felt like he'd been waiting years to marry her, not just a few days. And now that only an hour remained, each minute felt like a year.

A knock sounded at the door and Wesley let himself in. The groomsman had on a black suit, but he still looked rather lost. He clutched his little girl in his arms. She wore a pink woolen frock, but her golden hair hung loose and disheveled.

"Well, hello, little darling," Marguerite cooed to the child. "Can you come over here and see me?"

"You're pretty," Melissa told her. "You look like a fairy princess."

Cody glanced at his mother. Her pink skirt and pelisse combination did look quite nice on her. Melissa squirmed out of her father's embrace and ran to meet Cody's mother, who discreetly removed a tiny hairbrush from her reticule and began to put the messy locks in order.

"How are you doing, Wes?" Cody asked his friend. *It was asking a lot, requesting Wesley participate in this wedding so soon after his tragic loss.*

Wesley shook his head, indicating he wouldn't talk about it now. Cody honored the plea. "Where's Melissa going to sit?" he asked, changing the subject.

"With Becky," he replied. "Mother isn't coming."

Based on what Cody knew about Wesley's mother, this didn't upset him overly much. Besides, he really just wanted Kristina. He wanted to see her walking down the aisle, feel her arm in his, and hear her sweet voice saying her vows. *I want all this day represents and I don't want to wait for it another minute.* "Can't we just go?" he asked, hearing the whine in his voice, but finding himself unable to control it.

"You want to go into a room where a dozen women are decorating and hang around underfoot? Be my guest, son. I wouldn't do it if you paid me," Harold commented with a shudder.

"Let's go then," Cody said, ignoring his father's warning.

Marguerite approached, carrying Melissa. "This is the sweetest little girl, young man. You should be very proud of her," she said to Wesley.

"I am, ma'am. Believe me. She's..." Wesley gulped and didn't finish the sentence. Marguerite, being a sensitive soul, didn't press for anything more. Instead, she handed the neatly coiffed child back to her father. The group walked down the brick walkway, stepping carefully so as not to slip on a patch of hard-packed snow, and climbed the stairs to the church.

Inside, the flurry of activity seemed to have abated. A large group of women stood around admiring their work. Little bouquets consisting of a rose tied with a white ribbon adorned the end of each pew. The garland decorating the communion rail had been dotted with more bows. A table with a guest book and a long quill pen waited near the entrance. Cody sank onto the cushion nearest the stove and tuned out the world completely, remembering the night he'd slept with Kristina in his arms.

"Son." Cody jumped as his father shook his arm. "Sorry. They're ready to get started." Cody shook his head to clear away the memories. *Enough of the past, it's time to embrace the future.* He moved to the front of the church, reminding himself that for once, he would be in front of the pulpit, not behind it. Cody felt a presence behind him and glanced back to see Wesley, who seemed more lost than ever as he held his left wrist in his right hand, his eyes far away.

The organ let loose a blast, and Cody looked up, startled, but Kristina wasn't seated at the bench, of course. The teenage girl who'd played the angel in the Christmas cantata played a slow and uneven prelude on the intimidating instrument. Cody couldn't help but grin. Kristina must have been teaching her, but why were there people in the choir loft?

The question was answered when the girl rose from the bench and motioned to them. They stood and began singing "We Gather Together to Ask the Lord's Blessing."

Yes, that's exactly right. A marriage with the Lord as its foundation.

The hymn ended, and the girl moved to the piano bench and played again, this time processional music. Movement from the direction of the door caught Cody's eyes. Allison, dressed in pink, walked the length of the aisle and took her place opposite Wesley.

Then the moment for which he'd been so eagerly waiting arrived. *Kristina.* At last, she had arrived, and Cody couldn't tear his gaze from her face. His bride, clad in angelic white, clung to her father's arm as he escorted her towards him. James handed her to Cody, his Adam's apple bobbing convulsively as he walked up to the pulpit and took his place. Kristina took Cody's arm, and he placed his hand on top of hers. She trembled slightly, but her eyes sparkled with joy, and her lips remained curved in a sweet, shy smile.

In later years, Cody never could remember his wedding ceremony. He couldn't remember the words James said or the vows he made. The only memories he carried into his future were Kristina's beautiful eyes and the soft sound of her voice as she pledged her life to him.

He touched his lips chastely to hers, and color bloomed between the freckles on her cheeks. The next clear thought he had was facing the audience as James's booming voice intoned unsteadily, "Reverend and Mrs. Cody Williams."

Good thing I left off the corset, Kristina thought, realizing if her breath had been restricted, the sound of her new name might have just knocked her clean off her feet. As it was, her knees tried to give way and black spots swam across her field of vision. Cody must have felt her muscles go slack, because his hand tightened on her arm, supporting her as they walked slowly down the aisle.

At the back of the church, he helped her into her coat, the scarlet color set off beautifully against the shimmering white of her wedding garments. Outside, a wagon waited to drive them to the café. Cody lifted Kristina onto the seat under a shower of birdseed and joined her, taking her hand in his.

Billy Fulton, his face split in a wide grin, shook the reins, bells jingling, and the wagon rolled down the street. Cody's arm around Kristina's back warmed her through the fabric of her coat. She rested her cheek against his shoulder.

It took less than a minute to ride from the church to the café, and he helped her down again, taking her arm and escorting her into the warm, fragrant interior, where the counter had been transformed into a buffet. Owlishly, she blinked at the familiar room.

A single table remained—the least wobbly one of the bunch —covered with a cloth of snowy lace and set with a vase of pink silk roses.

Meats, cheese, fresh bread, dried fruit, and pastries, attractively arranged on white plates, lay scattered on a pink tablecloth, interspersed with artificial roses. In the center of the table sat a three-tiered cake in white frosting, with pink sugar roses and pale green sugar leaves clustered around the edges.

How pretty, Kristina thought, sending a wan grin to her friend. The pressure of Cody's arm in hers increased as he moved her in that direction. Passively, she moved at his urging. He helped her into a chair near the buffet table, and she sank into it gratefully, her knees still unsteady. She vaguely noticed the crowd of well-wishers pressing close to them on all sides. She smiled, but all her attention remained focused on Cody. *My husband.*

She clung to his arm, feeling strangely out of her depth among the people she had known her whole life. It was as though the world had somehow shifted around her and she no longer knew who they were or even who she was. *No longer Miss Kristina Heitschmidt, but who is Mrs. Cody Williams? I don't know. This new woman is someone I'll have to get used to. A new version of myself, with new responsibilities and new freedoms.* Her cheeks burned at the thought of those freedoms. Suddenly, after weeks of such intense longing, she no longer felt ready for what was certain to come tonight.

The guests, seeing the bride's blush, began making teasing remarks. Embarrassed, she hid her face against Cody's shoulder. This only made them tease more.

After a time, Cody walked her to Lydia's dark, rich fruitcake and they cut it. They fed each other little bites.

A crowd of young women gathered around, and she tossed her bouquet of hothouse roses straight to Allison, who, being a head taller than everyone else, caught them easily. *There. A good luck charm for my friend.*

"Well, friends, it seems the wedding feast has ended," Cody quipped, waving his hand at the decimated snack trays and fragments of cake, "so I suggest we all head home."

Raucous hoots and ribald suggestions greeted the pronouncement.

The burning in Kristina's face felt almost as violent as it had on the night of the blizzard. *The night when all this started, heaven help me.* Shaking her head in a vain attempt to ward off unruly thoughts, she let Cody lead her to the wagon, which took them to the vicarage. Cody thanked Billy and brought his wife inside, locking the door behind them.

Every movement felt strangely dreamlike, as though she had parted ways with reality. She turned slowly to face her husband, and some of the shock of the day seemed to pass off. As the haze faded into awareness, a strange sensation pooled in the pit of Kristina's stomach. *I married Cody. I've known him a month and I'm his wife. What was I thinking? This is madness.* Marry in haste, repent in leisure, so the saying went. And they had married in ridiculous haste. She gulped.

Cody crossed the room and took her hand gently in his, leading her to the sofa and urging her to sit.

"Are you all right, darlin'?" he asked her. "You look like a ghost."

"Do ghosts have freckles?" she quipped weakly.

Her trembling voice must have provided him an even greater clue to her mood and he crushed her in a hug. "It's all right. We're going to be fine."

"Huh?"

"You look like you're about to faint, Kristina."

"I never faint," she replied, steeling herself against the overwhelming thoughts that threatened to engulf her. She considered standing, but Cody's arms around her provided warmth and comfort, and she decided to stay cuddled there for a while.

This close, breathing in the scent of his skin, feeling the power of his embrace, she felt better. It all made sense again. *Yes, there will be adjustments, but he's a good man, and I'm a good woman. Surely our marriage can be made into something positive.*

And then he lifted her chin and lowered his mouth to hers, calming her further with a long, sweet kiss. Another followed, and then another. Cody pulled the pins from Kristina's hair, letting the strands fall long down her back. He ran his hands into the rippling sunset silk, cradling the back of her head and holding her still while he explored her mouth with his questing tongue.

This part she understood. Granting him access, she caressed his tongue with hers, tasting him back.

At last, he released her and drew in an unsteady breath. "Come with me," he told her, lifting her to her feet. The clock on the mantel read quarter after four, but the sun already hung low in the sky. Winter nights began early, and long shadows stretched across the floor of the vicarage as Cody led his bride to their marriage bed.

He pulled back the quilt to reveal a snowy sheet. A fine trembling began in Kristina's hands.

"I don't think I'm ready for this," she whispered.

"I know," he replied. "I didn't think you would be."

"You didn't?"

"Of course not. I mean, we've only known each other a short time, and you've spent most of your life assuming you would remain celibate. It's a radical change to make in a month, and we've been so good during this courtship. In a way, it's a bit of a setback."

She gave him a puzzled look. "How so?"

"Well, from what I've read, a lot of courting couples, even ones who wait for their wedding for the whole... consummation..." Cody's cheeks were beginning to look suspiciously pink. He sat on the bed and urged her to a seat beside him.

"What do they do, Cody?" she asked.

"Well, they take... liberties." His blush deepened.

"We took liberties," she said, thinking of all the passionate embraces they'd shared.

"No, Kristina, we didn't. We kissed. But we didn't... touch each other."

Her eyes widened. "You mean... intimately?" *Oh, this is difficult. My face must match my hair.*

"Yes. That's exactly what I mean. It's a lot to go from kissing to... everything in one day. So, um... I don't think we should."

"Shouldn't..." she couldn't finish.

"Shouldn't consummate the marriage... today." He blurted in a rush.

Relief blended with crushing disappointment. "You don't want...?"

"I do want, Kristina. I want you so bad, I think I'm going to burst." He took her hands in his and kissed each one.

"Then why..."

"I... well it's hard to put into words. I've never done this. Neither have you. And it's us, so I want it to be special. I don't want to... fumble all over you the first time. I think we need to... well, to practice a bit before we really... you know."

I really don't.

Her confusion must have shown on her face, because Cody said, "Listen, Kristina. I'm not talking about months here or even weeks. Just a few days to practice, to learn how to touch each other."

She dropped his hand and pressed her knuckles to her mouth. "Cody, what? I've always heard men were lusty creatures, forever in a hurry to take a lady to bed. Now you have every right to do so, and you're proposing to wait longer? Where did you get this idea from?"

He reached for the bureau beside the bed and lifted a book, handing it to her. "My old professor sent me this. I think he wrote it, even though his name isn't on it. It reads like his old lecture notes, at least in style. I never heard a lecture like this. It's about how to start a marriage right so both the husband and the wife learn to enjoy intimacy."

Kristina flipped through the pages. There were illustrations. She closed the book sharply, the covers slapping. *I will never, as long as I live, be able to remove that image from my mind.* She set the book back on the bureau, shaking her head. "And this book suggests postponing... the event?"

"Yes, in these circumstances. Obviously if one of us were widowed... had some experience... it would be easier, but neither of us knows what we're doing. It's a blessing that we can learn together, but it's going to take time to figure it all out. I don't want to hurt you or make you afraid. I'd rather we take our time. What's a few days, against our whole life together?"

There's sense in what he was saying. While she understood the basic mechanics of coupling, she had never considered the fact that it might be enjoyable for the woman. It seemed impossible. "Won't waiting be painful for you? What if you can't stand it anymore?"

"Well, that's the beauty of it, darlin'. If we can't wait anymore, we don't have to." He gave her a shy grin. "But there's a way you can... help me if things get too intense. I'll show you. Are you willing?"

"Willing to do what, precisely?"

"For now, willing to let me touch you in ways you've never been touched before. Help me understand what feels good to you. And you touch me. We learn together. No guilt, no sneaking around. Just a husband and wife taking their time coming together so it can be perfect."

Kristina licked her lips. "And if I don't like something you're doing?"

"You tell me, and I'll stop. And if you do like it, let me know so I'll keep going."

She nodded. "Yes. Okay. Sounds like a good plan. Where do we start?"

Cody kissed her gently and walked across to the sitting area where he retrieved his Bible. She quirked one eyebrow at him.

"Trust me, darlin'."

"I do. But, Cody..."

"Marital intimacy is a gift from God. Let me show you." He flipped through the pages to Song of Solomon and read several raw, passionate references to the Lover observing and then caressing the Beloved's body. He read of her impassioned response.

When he finished, Kristina's heart was pounding. She drew in an unsteady breath. This time, when Cody reached for her, she went into his arms eagerly, letting him press her down onto the mattress as one long, languorous kiss blended into another. Her hands came to rest on his chest, and she stroked them lightly up and down, feeling the firmness of his muscles.

Cody kept one arm wrapped around his wife's waist, but the other... the other trailed around her side, upwards, cupping one full plump breast, gently squeezing and shaping its softness.

Stimulated by his touch, the peak pebbled, rising against his palm. He grasped it between his fingertips and a sharp stab of pure, white-hot pleasure streaked through Kristina. She whimpered against his mouth. Her other nipple rose eagerly, and Cody moved his hand over to it, plucking in the same arousing manner. Stunned, Kristina pulled back from him.

"Stop," she urged.

"What, darlin'?"

"It can't be right. It feels too good."

He grinned. Then he quoted the verse he'd just read. "Thy stature is like to a palm tree, and thy breasts to clusters of grapes. I said, 'I will go up to the palm tree, I will take hold of the boughs thereof.' See, darlin'? If Solomon can do it, I can."

Kristina pondered his words in silence. *He's right, but I can scarcely imagine feeling a sensation like that.* Drawing a deep breath, she arched her back, pressing her lower body fully against his, noting the firm protuberance rubbing against the front of her skirt while she offered her breasts to his touch.

At her surrender, Cody's eyes lit with a sapphire flame. He threaded one hand into her hair and plundered her mouth with hot, wild kisses while his other hand made free with the tempting globes. He toyed with her nipples until she was gasping. Then he opened the brooch at her throat and began to work the buttons of her shirtwaist.

When the garment hung loose around her torso, he looked down, taking in the luscious sight of her large, lovely breasts filling up the top of her chemise. Through the thin white fabric, the pink of her nipples must be visible. The neck of the undergarment scooped, revealing the upper swells, speckles continuing down her neck and onto her bosom. He pressed his lips to each one.

His warm breath on her skin stoked the fire of Kristina's passion even higher. She felt like melted snow; puddled, liquid. The cold seeping in around the windows no longer chilled her. Not when her husband was touching her, kissing her so sweetly. He reached for the straps of her chemise and lowered the garment, baring the delicate flesh he'd just caressed so thoroughly. With unsteady hands, he cupped her breasts and lifted them, pressing a gentle kiss to each nipple.

"Ohhhh," Kristina sighed, and he took the touch further, lashing one pert peak with the tip of his tongue.

Her head fell back, offering him greater access.

He took it, nipping and sucking. Kristina squirmed against an unexpected tingle at the apex of her thighs. Instinctively, she knew Cody would be able to help her with it, and she ground herself against his body, seeking stimulation.

Cody knew what his wife wanted. He wanted to give it to her, but he had reached the limit of his control. *If I touch her there now, I'll be inside her in a moment and done about ten seconds later.*

"Kristina." His voice cut through her passion. She opened her eyes. "I need you. I can't go on like this any longer. Can you help me?"

"What do I do?"

In answer, Cody rose from the bed and began to remove his clothing. She watched, her eyes wide, but she didn't look away.

Good. She's curious. When he removed his undershirt, baring his chest, her eyes widened further. Then he lowered his drawers. She inhaled in shock at the sight of his fully erect sex.

"Oh, Cody. That's not going to work. It's too big."

"It'll be fine, darlin'. We'll go real slow, but not now. Come here." He finished removing her blouse and chemise, and then her skirt, leaving her clad only in her bloomers. Her freckled breasts enticed him. He touched her there again, teasing her nipples between his fingertips. Then he stretched out beside her and took her hand in his.

"Do you trust me?" he asked, looking deep into the drowning depths of her eyes. She nodded. He guided her hand to his erection and curled her fingers around it. She gasped. He groaned.

"What are you doing?" she asked in a tiny voice.

"Help me, Kristina. I... I need..." There were no words, so he showed her how to stroke him.

"Don't stop," he urged as he lifted his hands away.

She continued caressing him, thank God. He returned to cupping and nuzzling her breasts, sucking her nipples one after the other.

"Ahhhh," she sighed at the sweet stimulation.

"Don't stop," he begged, and she resumed her task. Cody groaned, and then his groan turned to a growl. His body went rigid, watching liquid splatter across her belly.

She watched, fascinated. Then her eyes returned to his face, taking in what must be an expression of intense relief.

Cody leaned over and kissed her forehead. "Did that bother you, darlin'?"

"No," she replied. "How could it? You look so happy."

"I am," he told her. "It was... amazing. You did an excellent job." He kissed her flaming cheek, and then returned to her lips. Then he retrieved a rag and wiped her skin clean.

"Sweet Kristina," he murmured, "it's your turn. I think you were looking for some relief too, weren't you?"

"Oh, I don't know..." she prevaricated

"Don't be shy. I want you to feel good." Cody opened the tie of her bloomers and lowered them, admiring her soft, cinnamon-sprinkled belly.

As though to compensate for her unfashionable face, Kristina had been blessed with a glorious figure. In addition to luscious full breasts, she also had a naturally small waist and round, curvy hips.

At his intense regard, her thighs clenched instinctively.

He didn't push her. Instead, he covered her body with his, letting her feel his weight. He treated her to another round of delicious kisses, sliding his tongue past her lips. He kissed her until her body relaxed under him. Then he let his hands rove over her again. Cody could feel her softening and opening. Quickly, he slipped his fingers into the space between her thighs, cupping her. She tried to close against him again, but he was entrenched.

"Relax, darlin'. You don't want me to stop now. Let me try and help you. You've been burning up for days, haven't you?"

"Weeks," she admitted.

"Then let me quench your fire. Open, Kristina. I'm your husband. Let me touch you."

She closed her eyes and let her thighs fall apart.

"Is she sleeping?" Wesley asked as Allison descended the stairs. He walked her into the parlor and urged her to sit on the sofa.

She grabbed his cup of hot tea and took a sip. "Yes. She's sleeping now."

"Thank you, Allison. I don't know if I could take another night of her crying for her mother." Wesley shook his head and retrieved his teacup from her hands.

She slipped her arm behind his back and hugged him. "I'm sorry."

He shrugged, but his expression remained bleak.

"How are you holding up?" she asked.

He shook his head, wriggling out of her embrace

"Come on, Wes. We've been friends forever. We used to be betrothed. Who else are you going to talk to?"

"I don't want to talk. I want to... do something. Anything. But what can I do? Sam is dead. She's dead, Allison. I failed her. I should have done more."

Allison laid a hand on his arm. "There's nothing more you could have done. She's gone. That part is over. You can't worry about her anymore. The question is, what are you going to do for Melissa and yourself?"

"Damned if I know," he replied. "I have to be back at work two days after Christmas. Melissa's three. She's not even in school yet. Who will watch over her while I'm at the bank? Who will cook and take care of the house? I don't even know how to do those things. What can I do, Allison? I'm barely hanging on now. If I have to be at work all day..."

"What about your mother?" she asked.

He gave her a telling look.

"I know, but at least she could watch over Melissa for a while as you figure out what's next."

"I already asked her." His neutral voice didn't bode well.

"She didn't refuse?"

He nodded. "She said she did her time taking care of a child and wasn't going to use her golden years to do more of the same."

"Wes, don't take this wrong, but I don't like your mother."

He turned towards her. "She doesn't like you either, Allison."

Allison shrugged. "It used to worry me, but I don't care anymore."

"Are you sure?" A note of intensity had developed in Wesley's voice. Allison gave him a questioning glance.

"I'm sure I no longer care whether your mother likes me. Our engagement ended four years ago when you married Samantha. Why on earth would her opinion matter to me now?"

"Well... no. Never mind." His eyes veered away from her face.

"What is it, Wes?" Allison placed her hand against his cheek and turned him back to face her.

"No, I can't, Allison."

"Wesley Fulton, for heaven's sake, speak! What is going through that mind of yours?"

"It's just... well... I need a wife, Allison. I can't work and raise my daughter and take care of the house alone. There are only two women in the world I trust with Melissa, and Kristina just got married so..."

"So?" Though her heart pounded, she couldn't believe he was really saying what she thought he was saying.

"So, would you consider... reinstating our betrothal?"

She blinked. "You mean when your year of mourning is up?"

"No. That's too long, I need you now. I need this to be your home, and for you to be here with me. I need you after Christmas, to care for Melissa when I go back to the bank. Hell, I need you before Christmas so her first holiday without her mother isn't a total disaster."

She looked at him, stunned.

"I know it's a lot to ask, but would you consider it, Allison? I need you."

She shook her head, not to say no, but as though to clear it, and put her hands over her face. "When?" she croaked.

"Tomorrow? Sunday? Whenever Cody can do it."

"Oh, Lord, Wes. You want the pastor to perform a wedding the day after his own?" She dissolved into hysterical giggles.

He turned away and regarded the window. She pulled him back around again, making him look into her eyes. "Yes, Wesley."

His jaw dropped, and he rubbed his ears as though hearing a strange sound. "Yes?"

"Yes. On one condition."

Wesley rubbed his jaw and temples. "What condition?"

"It has to be a real marriage. I refuse to be your glorified housekeeper. It's all or nothing, Wes." Her cheeks burned at the bold statement, but he had to understand there were no other options.

"Are you sure you want to do this?" he asked her.

"Oh yes," she replied. "I agreed to marry you five years ago. A year later I lost you. Now that I have this opportunity, I'm not letting you go."

Wesley nodded.

"But if you go to bed with another woman, ever again..."

"I won't. I swear!" He grabbed her and kissed her. She kissed back with equal fervor. *At last, after all these years of suffering and grief, the man I love will finally be mine.*

Chapter Thirteen

S aturday afternoon, Cody walked up the brick walkway to the church and plunked down in a pew, notepad and pencil in hand. He appropriated a pew Bible and started leafing through the Old Testament.

Newlywed or not, there will be a sermon to preach tomorrow, and it's the last Sunday in Advent. He wasn't ready. For the moment at least, working at home was proving impossible. He'd tried, but listening to Kristina bustle around—rearranging his pots and pans, tidying the house, humming all the while—had proved far too distracting.

His mind remained bathed in images of her naked body, spread out in bed while he touched and tasted her. He could still hear the soft noises she'd made when he finally got her to climax. It was a much more difficult task than he'd expected, but he'd persevered and succeeded in the end. And then, the moment both of them had relaxed, his hand had accidentally brushed her breast, and they'd started the entire process over again. *At this rate, we'll be experts in a week.*

After a long night of love play, they'd slept late, and now Cody *had to* prepare his sermon for tomorrow.

Isaiah. Yes. I'll use Isaiah. And John. Save Matthew for

Christmas Eve. Good. What hymns? Kristina will pick the hymns, but I need scriptures and an outline for her to work with.

"Lord, what do I preach on?" Cody asked, "I can't concentrate. Help me."

The Lord answered Cody in a way he did not expect. The door of the church banged open and Wesley Fulton barged in, flopping gracelessly onto the scarlet pew cushion beside him.

"Hello, Wes," Cody said archly, not in the mood to be interrupted.

"Cody, I need your help."

Cody considered his friend's expression and tone. *There's something different about Wes this afternoon. Instead of despairing, he seems... terrified.*

"What do you need?" Cody asked.

"I need your professional services."

"As counselor?"

"No, as pastor. I need to get married. Right away."

Cody raised an eyebrow. "Has Miss Spencer agreed to this?"

Wesley's jaw dropped. "How did you know?"

"Who else would it be? Listen, Wes, I don't think it's a good idea. Your wife just died. You need your season of mourning before you go on with your life. Take the time."

"I can't," Wesley insisted. "I need a mother for Melissa."

"Other widowed fathers have gotten through, Wes," Cody told him. "You can too."

"I can't. I don't know the first thing about caring for a little girl. And I can't watch over her and provide for her at the same time. I need a wife. Allison is willing. Please?" he begged.

Cody made a face. "You do realize, don't you, you're proposing a marriage of convenience to the woman who loves you?"

"Yes." Wesley's dark eyes turned downward.

"Don't you think it's a little unfair to her?" Cody said the harsh words as gently as he could.

"I know it. I'm a selfish bastard, but I need Allison. Please, Cody. Please do this for us."

"Us?" Cody snorted. "Sounds more like do this for you. What is Miss Spencer getting out of it? You're asking her—for the rest of her life—to give up on finding a husband who loves her. Doesn't she deserve that?"

Wesley sat in silence for a long moment. When he spoke, the words cut straight to Cody's heart. "Doesn't Kristina?"

"We are *not* talking about Kristina," Cody replied, letting a hint of anger bleed into his voice, "but for the record, she doesn't need to look for one. She has one."

"Good," Wesley replied. Then he added. "I think the potential is there, in time. I mean, I was betrothed to her before, and it had nothing to do with convenience. I just... right now..."

"So, you're telling me you want to marry her now because you loved her before and you hope to be able to again, once you pull yourself together?"

"Something like that." Wes had the grace to sound sheepish.

Cody sighed. "Miss Spencer must be an absolute saint."

"She is."

Cody considered the strange request. He knew such things happened—widowed parents remarried with undue haste to provide the missing family member for their child. In this case, Melissa would benefit. He'd seen the little girl with Miss Spencer, and they were comfortable together. *There are worse fates than growing up with Allison Spencer for a mother.*

Wesley would also benefit, of course, from a beautiful, smart wife, but Cody still had to think about what was best for the bride. "I need to talk to her before I decide. Where is she?"

"Having tea with your wife. We looked for you there, first."

"Ah, I see." Cody sighed. The sermon would have to wait until later. "Let's go back to the vicarage and talk, the four of us."

"Okay." Wesley hauled himself to his feet. Cody noticed his clothing was dirty and his hair disheveled. *He isn't exaggerating when he says he needs a wife.*

Cody gathered his materials and followed his friend out of the church and back through the biting December cold to his home, where, as expected, the two ladies sat on the sofa sipping tea while little Melissa devoured a cookie at the table.

"Hello, darling," Kristina called out to Cody cheerfully, but he could see the worry in her eyes. *She's no keener on this plan than I am.*

"Mrs. Williams." He leaned down and touched his lips to her cheek, enjoying the sight of her blush for a moment before taking a seat in one armchair. Wesley perched in the other.

"Well," Cody said, "does everyone know what's going on?"

"Yes," Kristina replied, "Allison has been filling me in. What do you think?"

"I think there are some potential problems with this scenario," Cody replied soberly, "but I'm not going to give my opinion until I've heard from the bride in question. Miss Spencer, can you please tell me your take on all this?"

"It's simple. I want to marry Wesley. What more is there to say?"

Cody laid it all out for her. "You want to marry him, knowing he's still grieving his wife, knowing he's in... a bad state. You're willing to take him on as-is, daughter in tow, *and* with a mother who doesn't like you?"

"Yes." She folded her hands in her lap and challenged Cody with a direct stare.

"Why?"

"There's nothing I would refuse Wesley. This is not the worst thing he could have asked me." She lifted her head and turned away from him to meet Wesley's eyes.

"What do your parents say?"

She returned her attention to Cody. "I haven't asked them. I'm twenty-four years old, Reverend Williams. I want to get married and my best friend has asked me. I'd like it done as soon as possible."

"How soon?"

"Tomorrow."

China rattled. Apparently, she had not informed Kristina of that part of the plan yet. His wife righted her overturned cup and rose, carrying it over to the sink.

He watched her go, unable to tear his gaze from her lovely round backside. *We have to get this resolved. The delay is preventing me from getting my sermon done, which prevents me from caressing my wife some more.* Cody wanted to groan with frustration.

Kristina returned, but instead of sitting next to Allison, she stood behind Cody's chair and laid a hand on his shoulder. The moment he realized the space was unoccupied, Wesley jumped into it, taking Allison's long-fingered hand in his.

Cody looked at the couple coolly. He had grave misgivings about the circumstances of this marriage, but he acknowledged that as adults, they had the right to make the decision. *There's no good reason for me to refuse, and their matching expressions of determination tell me if I don't do this, they'll make it happen some other, less appropriate way.*

Cody turned away from them, his gaze moving toward the dining table.

"Melissa," he called. The little girl raised her head and looked at him. Crumbs dropped from her lips and chin with the movement. "Can you come here please?"

She scrambled down and ran across the room, climbing onto his lap. He brushed the remaining bits of cookie from her face.

"How are you, Melissa?" he asked.

"I miss Mommy," she replied.

"I know, and it's very sad. How would you like a new mommy?"

The child considered. "Can it be Auntie Allie?"

Cody sighed. That question told him everything he needed to know. "Yes, Melissa. It can be."

Chapter Fourteen

Christmas Eve dawned bright but desperately cold. Cuddled under the quilt with Cody's arms around her, Kristina felt quite fine, except for one thing. Three days into their marriage, she was—embarrassingly—still a virgin.

Not that she was chaste, far from it. They'd spent each night 'practicing', but had yet to take the final step. *I'm not afraid anymore, in fact, I'm more than ready.*

She snuggled back against him. His warmth felt so lovely against her body. Even in his sleep, she could feel his arousal, firm and thick against her bottom. *I hope it won't hurt too much.* A thrill of nerves coursed through her. *I want the initiation over with.*

Despite the distraction, he'd managed to put together a fine sermon for yesterday. And then, against everyone's better judgment, he'd performed a wedding ceremony for Wesley and Allison. Kristina could still hear Mrs. Spencer shrieking when she arrived at the church ten minutes too late to stop it.

Now that she was awake, Kristina needed the necessary. *Drat.* She wriggled out of Cody's embrace and hurried out to the outhouse in her nightgown, nearly freezing her feet. *I can't wait to get a water closet installed. That will be a priority in our proposed expansion of the house.*

By the time she slipped back into bed with her husband, she had grown thoroughly chilled, and she burrowed into Cody's warmth. One of her icy feet touched his bare ankle, and he stirred, hugging her. His lips touched the back of her neck and his hands slid up her torso to cup her breasts.

"Hmmmm." She hummed at the pleasure of his touch. Her nipples were already rock-hard from the cold. Even half-awake, he found them and gripped them, rolling the little nubs between his fingertips. His body arched, grinding his sex into her bottom.

"Cody?"

"Yes, darlin'?"

She rolled in his arms, so she could look deep into his beautiful blue eyes. "Don't stop. Promise me. Not this time."

She waited for some insouciant remark about her eagerness, but he offered none. "I won't," he said simply. Then he pulled her close and laid a kiss on her mouth.

He slept in only in his drawers, and within moments, he had guided Kristina's hand inside them.

"Cody?"

"Trust me. I'm way too close, but this doesn't mean I'm stopping." He shoved off the covers, pulled the garment down and pushed all the fabric aside with one foot.

She trusted him, and so she stroked his sex in the way she'd learned he liked, until he groaned in sweet release, his seed spilling onto the rag she'd retrieved from its new home under the edge of the bed.

"Oh, that's so good, darlin'. Now I have some time to work on you."

He lifted her nightgown over her head and urged her down on her back, leaning over her. He kissed her again and again, and, while holding his weight with one hand, let the other roam over her luscious curves. He thumbed one plump pink nipple and drew the other into his mouth, sucking and tugging in the way he'd learned was sure to set her on fire.

Cody aroused his bride slowly, making her body burn until her hips began to squirm involuntarily. Then he slid his hand down over the softness of her belly, down to the thatch of red curls that guarded her womanly secrets. Secrets he'd been learning, little by little.

Their hours of love play had melted away her shyness, and Kristina no longer clamped her thighs together against the touch of his fingers. She opened eagerly, loving the way he parted the lips and delved into her dewy folds.

Cody smiled as Kristina made one of those sweet pleasure noises that told him he was touching her the right way. It changed all the time, what his wife wanted, and he'd learned to read her responses rather than trying to follow some kind of routine. But there was a rhythm to pleasuring his lady.

Wet the fingers. Always wet fingers there; the flesh is too delicate for anything else. But she was responsive and easily aroused, and finding moisture to spread over her never posed a problem. He slipped one finger inside, found the opening in her hymen and slipped past it, probing deeper. He imagined what all that soft wet flesh would feel like. *Before much longer, I'll know.*

He grew instantly hard again. Cody sucked his breath in. *Kristina. Focus on Kristina. Pleasure your wife.* He withdrew his finger and returned with two, passing the little barrier again, but this time stretching her, trying to prepare her body to receive him. His thumb worked upwards to a tender spot he'd found.

What did the book say? Touch it gently, as though you were stroking the wings of a butterfly. She likes it when I do that. Feathery caresses elicited another sobbing gasp.

He sat up a bit and looked down over the beauty of his wife as her pleasure built. Her hands fisted in the sheets, her sunset hair spread across the pillow, her lush, curvaceous figure all splayed out in front of him, modesty forgotten, every last freckle on display. *She's glorious.*

And then she clamped down, cries of pleasure ripped from her throat as even more moisture surged. "Oh, Cody. Ahhhh."

He slipped his fingers out of her and positioned himself atop her body. She wrapped her arms around his shoulders, her gaze filled with desire. He planted his knees on the bed, holding the bulk of his weight off her with one arm while the other closed around his sex, guiding it into position.

He kissed her and rolled his hips forward. She opened her thighs wider in welcome, but the entrance to her body resisted. *She's so tight. She has to relax, or I'll hurt her.*

"Kristina," he said, and she opened her brilliant blue-green eyes and regarded him solemnly. "Are you ready for me?" He eased in the first scant inch.

"Yes, Cody. I'm ready." He progressed to her maidenhead and nudged against it.

"Be my wife." He pushed. It refused to yield.

She winced. "I am your wife."

Cody leaned down and pressed his lips to hers, distracting her again as he increased the pressure.

The membrane gave way. Kristina gasped against his mouth.

"For this reason, a man shall leave his father and mother and be joined to his wife, and the two shall become one flesh." He slid deeper, giving her his innocence, taking hers unto himself.

Kristina had gone utterly limp under his body. She lay passive as he filled her to the limit of her capacity.

"Are you all right?" he asked her when at last his forward movement stopped.

She inhaled shakily. "Um, yes. I think so."

"We've done it."

She nodded.

Despite his earlier release, Cody was one thrust away from completion. The sensation of her wet, tight heat proved to be more than he could bear, so he stayed still, memorizing this moment.

Then he pulled back and thrust, and the glorious friction brought him the most powerful orgasm he'd experienced to date.

❦

Kristina stroked her husband's back as burning liquid spilled into her belly. She was stinging a bit still, and the fullness startled her, though it waned as his erection faded. Now Cody fell limp, collapsing on top of her.

She touched her lips to his whisker-roughened cheek. *What an interesting experience.* She had enjoyed most of it. *Once I'm used to it, I'm sure it will be fine.*

He slipped out of her, and her intimate flesh throbbed and ached. She felt stretched and slightly wounded. She was considering her feelings, whether she wanted to cry, when her husband rolled off her and gathered her into his arms.

With tender kisses, he soothed her overwrought emotions as he positioned her for cuddling. He kissed the top of her head. She touched her lips to his chest.

"Did that feel good to you?" she asked softly.

"Oh yes," Cody replied, "wonderful. Next time I want it to be wonderful for you, too."

"I know it will be," she replied.

After long minutes of cuddling, she realized she could hear Cody's stomach growling. Her hunger gnawed at her.

"Would you like some breakfast?" she asked him.

"Sure, darlin'," he replied.

She found her abandoned nightgown where it had been tossed among the tangled sheets and pulled it over her head. Then she climbed out of bed, making a soft protesting sound as her feet touched the icy floorboards again.

"Hold on, Kristina." Cody reached over to the bureau and

pulled out a pair of thick knitted socks. "Put these on." He tossed them to her.

The fuzzy gray didn't excite her, but she needed the warmth, and with the startling amount of fluid left behind in the aftermath of their consummation, she was not about to dress until she'd had a bath.

Lighting the cook stove, she set a kettle and a pot of water on to boil and soon had coffee and porridge ready for the two of them. As she worked, she kept glancing back at Cody. He luxuriated in the bed a little longer before rising, hunting down his drawers and undershirt, and slipping them back on. He added a blue-striped dressing gown for warmth and dug a pair of house shoes out from under the bed to cover his long, narrow feet.

His movement revealed a mark on the sheets. Not a large one, but quite visible. Smears of blood mingled with other fluids. Kristina fought back a sniffle. *It was inevitable,* she reminded herself fiercely. *Did you truly* want *to die a virgin?*

She didn't—and now she wouldn't—but the momentousness of the act would not be denied. It crept over her while she busied herself setting the table for two. The two clean spoons she carried dropped to the floor as she brought her hands up over her face.

Cody vaulted up from his crouch in an instant and crossed the room in two long-legged strides. He hugged her close, asking no questions, making no comments, just stroking her back with one strong hand while the other pressed her cheek against his shoulder.

He held her for a few minutes while she gave vent to her confused emotions. Then, when the storm had passed, he tilted her face up and kissed her forehead, chin, and lips.

"Shall we eat?" he asked, and she realized he had no idea what to say next.

"Yes, let's," she replied, "There's no point in letting a hot breakfast get cold just because I'm being silly."

He took her hand. "Kristina," he told her seriously, "you weren't being silly."

She nodded, and he escorted her to the table, retrieving the abandoned spoons and dropping them in the sink before collecting two more from the drawer.

He handed her one and sat beside her, taking her hand again and asking a quick blessing over the breakfast.

They ate without speaking, Kristina still contemplating the events of the morning, and how she felt about them. She wasn't sure what exactly was going through Cody's head, but his gaze fell on her frequently. She could feel his blue eyes like a physical touch. Sometimes he did touch her, running a finger down her cheek, taking her hand and squeezing it gently, or touching his lips to her face.

The sting was fading now, and as her body adjusted to having been deflowered, curiosity rose moment by moment. *Will it always feel so strange? Will I really come to enjoy... that?*

She ate the last bite of her porridge, sipped her tepid coffee and turned fully towards her husband, to find his eyes on her again. She stood, reaching out, sliding her arms around his neck and perching herself on his knee.

"Cody, you did a good job. You were right about the practicing. That was as nice a first time as a girl could ask for."

He grinned, but there was a hint of regret in it. "I hurt you."

"Not nearly as much as I expected," she replied, "and it wasn't you. It was just the nature of these things. What you did was make the rest of it lovely."

Heat flared in his expression and she could see the long moments of caressing playing in front of his eyes.

She leaned down and boldly touched her lips to his. "Do you think we could pull in the bathtub? I need to... clean up."

He nodded. His power of speech, it appeared, had failed.

"I'll heat the water."

As Kristina set about the arduous task of heating enough water to bathe in, Cody exited through the back door and returned, lugging the ridiculously heavy porcelain bathtub that lived in the backyard as it was too bulky to be kept in such a small house. Again, Kristina looked forward to the day when this place could be remodeled. Running water and a room for the bathtub to reside in sounded perfect. For the moment, they had to rely on this allegedly portable monstrosity and water heated on the stove.

Filling the tub took forever, but at last, it was ready. Kristina tested the water with her fingertips. *Perfect.* She found her little basket of soaps in one cabinet, and a stack of luxurious terry towels Rebecca Spencer had made for them as a wedding gift. Setting them near the tub, she crossed to her wardrobe and laid out her clothing for the day. Green skirt, white blouse, undergarments and stockings. Then she pulled her nightgown over her head.

Cody made a sound. She turned to find him staring at her naked body without a hint of shame.

A flush suffused her skin from head to toe.

"Darlin'," he said, his voice husky, "would you think me too forward if I asked to join you? The tub is big enough for two if we stay close."

She considered. He had already seen and touched every inch of her body, and in their life together, would do so again and again.

"Yes, of course," she replied. Since she was already at the wardrobe, she selected a suit of clothes for him to wear and laid them out on the bed beside hers. The rumpled sheets didn't please her, but she would make the bed when they were done.

By the time she crossed the room to the tub, Cody sat in it already, leaning against the back. He took her hand and helped her in. The space, which had seemed sufficient for two when empty, looked quite different with him in it. The only place for her to sit was on his lap. She knelt facing him, her legs on either side of his, and lowered her body down, sighing at the warmth of the water and determined not to be embarrassed by the intimate position.

Lifting a cup, she wet her husband's hair. Then she rubbed soap into her hands and washed him. Cody's eyes slid closed. *He*

155

must like this touch, she thought as she rinsed the soap from his hair. He took the cup from her hands and returned the favor, and it did feel nice, his big fingers scrubbing gently.

They took turns rubbing soap over each other's bodies. What started as practical quickly became sensual, washing fading into caressing. Kristina was beginning to feel aroused again, and if the phallus pressing against her provided any indication, her husband had reached that point long ago. *But am I ready for more?* A quick mental inventory told her the ache inside her had faded. *Maybe...*

But why rush? Kristina shifted to sit, her back leaning against the opposite wall of the tub, her thighs positioned along the outside of Cody's flanks. They regarded each other.

"You look so pretty like that," he told her, reaching across to touch her breasts, where they rested on top of the water. He thumbed her nipples and her eyes slid shut with the pleasure of the touch.

"Hmmm," she hummed as he caressed her. His hand dipped under the water, sliding along her torso. She wanted his touch and opened her thighs as wide as the walls of the tub would allow. He slipped his fingers between the folds and found what he had been seeking.

Her tiny nub responded eagerly to his touch, sending jolts of pleasure through Kristina's body. But somehow it wasn't enough. *I want... I need, more.*

She wasn't sure where the boldness came from, but she reached down and took his sex in her hand. The lower parts of their bodies were separated only by inches, and she positioned him, slowly feeding him inside her.

Cody groaned. "Aren't you sore, darlin'?"

"A little," she admitted, "but I still want this."

Cody let Kristina set the pace, flexing her body so he nudged deep inside her, squirming until she found a spot that provided the stimulation she craved while minimizing the sting.

He kept his fingers on her, increasing her pleasure with

feather-light touches on her most sensitive spot. Despite the hint of soreness, their loving felt like heaven. Kristina floated on a wave of pleasure. And then discomfort disappeared and all became white-hot ecstasy. In the distant part of her that still retained some awareness, she heard Cody's groan of pleasure as his peak coincided with hers.

Kristina returned to awareness slowly. *Warmth, peace, joy.* She felt a happiness she had scarcely imagined before. *Cody. Husband. Sweet loving.* She opened her eyes. Sunlight spilled across the floor, across the tub, illuminating her naked curves. Cody was looking at her.

She sighed a deep and languorous sigh. "Do you think I'm a hussy lying here nude in the sunlight?"

"No," he said, taking her question seriously. "It's like the Garden of Eden. I think... I think God made us for each other. There's no call for shame. Not when it's the two of us."

"Hmmm. So, this is Paradise? I think I might agree."

"Eve must have looked like you."

"With freckles?"

"Of course. She was naked in the sun all day. She was also the image of temptation, just like you tempt me." He shifted his position, covering her body with his and kissing her. She returned his kiss eagerly, opening to the request of his tongue.

She has no idea how special she is, Cody thought. *I'm blessed to have her. To watch innocence give way to eagerness... no, that's wrong. Her innocence is not damaged by this. It's no sin.*

His sex, still wedged inside her, tried to rise, but in the wake of three orgasms, it proved impossible. He slipped from her body.

"How sore are you now?" he asked.

She shrugged. "No worse. I think the way you went about it was good."

"No regrets?"

"Cody," she looked up into his eyes, "what could there possibly be for me to regret?"

That earned her another kiss. Then Cody disentangled himself from her limbs and stood, grabbing the towel to dry himself off. He stepped from the tub.

Kristina stretched, savoring the cooling water for another few minutes before rising. She seated herself by the fire and ran the brush through her hair.

Cody emptied the tub, one bucketful at a time, trying to avoid spilling the water on the path to the outhouse. He didn't want ice to form there, and the temperature remained well below freezing. Then he dragged the heavy tub back outside. Returning, he found his wife still on the sofa, naked, her long red hair spilling down around her back.

He wanted her again, but his stamina had finally given out. *Perhaps tonight.*

In the meanwhile, he enjoyed a lingering appraisal of her curves. At last, she rose, walked sinuously across the room to the bed, and began to dress. There was a new sensuality to her movements, an awakening of latent passion that suffused her. And then, just like that, it dissipated. The everyday clothing rendered her respectable Kristina... Williams again. *Well, almost. There's still something different about her.*

He watched her make the bed, tucking the sheets in with practiced efficiency, smoothing out the blankets and leaving no sign of the momentous event that had taken place there.

A knock sounded at the door. Kristina shot a glance at her husband and found him casually dressed in a pair of brown trousers and a loose white shirt, but no collar or tie. He had sprawled on the sofa to peruse a book and looked relaxed and happy. Kristina smiled and opened the door.

"Dad!" She wrapped her arms around James and squeezed

him right there at the door before ushering him inside and closing it against the late December chill. "Can I get you a cup of coffee?"

"Yes, please!" he agreed eagerly, and she hurried to comply while he took a seat on one of the armchairs adjacent to Cody.

"Hello, sir." Her husband smiled, but Kristina noticed an odd note in his voice. She approached with steaming mugs of dark, unsweetened brew for the two of them and saw Cody had sat up straight, his dark brows scrunching with discomfort.

She handed her father his cup. James's eyes dart around the room. Then he colored.

Oh dear, he was looking at the bed. Kristina risked a glance, horrified to think she'd left some tell-tale evidence of the goings-on there, but saw nothing. The covers lay perfectly smooth. It must have been the knowledge of what husbands and wives do together in beds that had embarrassed her father. Her cheeks burned at the thought. *Interior walls will be at the top of the priority list, right after water closets. Guests do not need to look at my bed.*

"So," she said, her voice overly bright, "what brings you this way, Dad?"

"Just wanted a pay a visit. It's Christmas Eve, and, well, I was lonely."

He isn't used to living alone, Kristina realized. *He needs company. Maybe even a wife.*

After three years as a widower, if he wanted to find a new companion, Kristina was in favor of it. The thought of Lydia immediately crossed her mind. The baker and restaurateur might be a little young, being only just past thirty while James had recently celebrated his forty-fifth birthday, but the plump, pretty, cheerful woman always had a sweet smile for him.

Kristina decided to make some discreet inquiries and see if Lydia had any interest. She'd make a fine addition to the family. Then it occurred to Kristina what her father's remarriage would mean, and her cheeks heated.

"This little place is quite cozy," James commented idly,

breaking the contemplative silence. "It must be nice to have such a small house to heat."

"It helps," Kristina replied, glad to think of something else. She poured the last of the coffee into a cup for herself and joined her husband on the sofa. He placed his hand on top of hers and just rested it there. It struck Kristina how shy he was acting. He'd never hesitated to kiss her cheek or put his arm around her shoulders in front of James before. It appeared everyone felt awkward this morning.

"So," Cody said, trying to divert attention away from the uncomfortable tension, "did everyone read yesterday's paper?"

Kristina noticed for the first time that when Cody was nervous, his Texas drawl become more pronounced. "I glanced at it in passing but didn't notice much. We're getting a new dress shop."

Both men gave her one of those looks, the one men give women when they say something hopelessly girly and uninformed. "What?" she demanded of them. "Allison's parents have taken out a mortgage to construct a store front for Becky beside the Sheriff's office. I'm so proud of the way she's taking charge of her future."

"Darlin', no one's putting down Becky or her ambitions," Cody explained, "but I was talking about the train robbery."

"Oh, dear. Another one? It wasn't your parents' train, was it?" Kristina touched the smooth milky stone of her wedding ring with the tip of her thumb. *I like Cody's parents so much. I would hate it if something bad happened to them.*

"No, they're all right as far as I know," Cody replied. "They should be home any time now. This train was between Dodge City and here. It was the closest robbery so far."

"Sheriff Brody must be about out of his mind with worry. He only has two deputies. They're all excellent at what they do, but even together they're not enough to take on a whole gang of train robbers." James looked grim. "Makes me want to rethink this..."

He extended his hand, offering an envelope to the couple.

Kristina took it and opened the flap. Inside, she discovered two slips of thick, cream-colored paper. "Train tickets?"

"Yes. I know it's been hard on you two, having to stay here and try to act normal so soon after your wedding. I remember what it's like... you just want to be alone together." James's cheeks turned a brilliant shade of crimson. "So, at any rate, I bought you two tickets to Wichita and reserved you three nights in a hotel room there... for a wedding trip. You leave the 26th on the early train."

Kristina sat blinking in surprise for several moments. Cody, it appeared, had also been rendered speechless.

"I thought," James continued, "you might be able to take in a concert or something. I heard there might be a traveling musical group in Wichita."

"Oh, Dad, thank you!" Kristina finally overcame her surprise and jumped up to hug her father.

"You're welcome, honey."

"Yes, thank you, sir," Cody added.

"What's this 'sir' business?" James asked, "I'm your father-in-law. It had better be James to you, if not Dad."

Cody opened his mouth and then shut it with a snap. "All right," he mumbled weakly.

Kristina went back to her husband, perching beside him and lacing her fingers through his. *He's worried*, she realized, *that Dad will object to our lovemaking.* It was as impossible to ignore as a buffalo in the room. She wondered how on earth she was going to handle all the knowing looks at church this evening. Instead of contemplating the birth of Christ, they'd be thinking about the pastor's private business. *Oh, this is just terrible!*

"Um, should we have lunch at Lydia's?" she suggested. "I don't have much to work with at the moment. Everything here is for tomorrow's dinner."

"I can't imagine you making one of your holiday dinners in this tiny kitchen," James commented. "Would you be agreeable to having dinner at my house instead?"

"Are you inviting me to eat, provided I do the cooking?" Kristina teased, a genuine smile spreading across her face.

"Something like that," James replied sheepishly. "What do you say, Cody?"

"It's fine by me," Cody said. "But as for lunch, is Lydia even open Christmas Eve?"

"Let's find out," Kristina said. "I feel like moving around a bit." *Actually, I just want Dad out of the house. I'm not ready for visitors yet.*

So, they all bundled up in as many layers as they could manage and made the chilly walk down Main Street, past ice-frosted brick buildings that sparkled in the bright, ineffective sunlight. The little café was indeed open, though only a handful of patrons sat at the wobbly tables.

"Hello, all!" Lydia called to them cheerfully as she bustled out of the kitchen with a steaming plate in each hand. It appeared pot roast was on the menu today, much heartier fare than Lydia normally served. She set one plate down in front of a man with salt-and-pepper hair and a thick mustache. The other she placed across the table from him.

"Be right back, Dylan," Kristina could barely hear Lydia's words to the sheriff. He nodded, and she hurried into the kitchen, bringing out three heaping plates of tender beef in gravy with root vegetables. On the side of each was one of Lydia's signature rolls, still warm from the oven. A heavenly fragrance wafted over the table.

As Cody bowed his head to ask a quick blessing, Kristina dared steal a glance through her eyelashes at Lydia and managed to catch her giving Sheriff Brody a look of heart-wrenching longing.

So much for matchmaking. Kristina turned her attention to the prayer.

As they devoured the succulent lunch, Kristina listened to the quiet hum of conversation around them. The words *train robbers* popped up frequently. By listening, she learned the gang was becoming more confident and more violent. In the last robbery, they'd shot the conductor and two young men who'd tried to protest. One had died.

"Do you have anything special planned for the service?" James asked, drawing Kristina's attention back to him.

"Special, but not new. Solemn Christmas carols provided by your lovely daughter," Cody clasped her hand, "interspersed with Bible readings. Candlelight. Then home to bed."

That hadn't come out right. The three diners flushed at the unintended reference.

They turned their attention to their last bites of beef, before leaving to walk back to the church. James left them at the door with a quick hug for each.

Alone again, the newlyweds treated each other to an indiscreet kiss before Kristina mounted the steps to the balcony and seated herself at the organ. The hymns were all familiar, of course. She'd learned to play "Away in a Manger" when she was seven, all the others in the intervening years. She'd practiced them for hours, performed them a dozen or more times, and yet today, each one had been made new.

Or rather she played them with a new passion, having discovered a depth of feeling in herself she had not been aware existed. Being awakened to human love had increased her understanding of the Divine. *It's just like the scripture Cody showed me; the one that described how marital intimacy was a symbol of Christ's love for the church. I've never understood it before.*

Now, having given herself in love to her husband, it began to become clear. *There's nothing I wouldn't do for Cody. He's everything to me. I love him more than my own life.* Kristina smiled. *And he loves me. I know it. I don't know why he does, but he does. We're blessed.*

Chapter Fifteen

Quarter till seven. People would be arriving soon. The lamps glowed soft and low. The candles on the Christmas tree glittered cheerfully among the ornaments, their glow adding to the gentle light, creating a setting for contemplation and reverence.

A blast of icy air hit Kristina. She turned to the open door and saw the first arrivals, the young Fulton family. Allison carried Melissa perched on her hip. The little girl wore a red dress and white mittens. A fur-lined hood kept her head warm. It struck Kristina how much Melissa looked like her stepmother, so much so, she could have been hers by blood. *Fitting, as Allison will likely be the only mother Melissa remembers.*

Allison set the child on the floor near the door and began unbuttoning her coat. Then Wesley took off his coat, hung it on one of the many hooks inside the door and scooped up his daughter. He took the girl to a seat near the front, off to one side. Melissa yawned hugely and laid her head on her father's shoulder. Allison approached Kristina and the two women hugged. Allison had a funny look on her face. Happy but embarrassed. Kristina knew what it meant. They burst into slightly hysterical giggles.

"You too?" she asked.

Allison nodded and bit her lip.

"Was it anything like what you expected?" Kristina asked. It was an improper question, but she didn't care.

"No," Allison said, and giggled again. "Who could imagine such a thing?" Her cheeks bloomed pink in the dim firelight.

In a way, knowing her friend was in the same boat made Kristina feel better about the whole thing. Not that it was a hardship exactly, just new and sometimes awkward.

The women hugged again, and then more parishioners tumbled into the room as though pushed by the driving Kansas wind, and the indiscreet conversation had to end. Allison took her seat beside her husband. He slipped his arm behind her back and the easy affection between them gave Kristina hope for the future of their marriage.

She looked up to see Cody standing beside her. *We'll never really be able to enjoy sitting together during a church service like most married couples do.*

He took her hand and squeezed it gently. The warm, tender look in his eyes promised more affection later. She stroked his fingers with her thumb and then climbed up the stairs and took her seat to begin the prelude with the haunting "What Child is This," a relatively new hymn with lyrics only twenty years old, set to an ancient tune. The minor key added a note of melancholy, reminding the congregation that the story ended at the cross, not the cradle.

This will be a Christmas worth remembering.

Chapter Sixteen

K ristina turned from looking out the train window. Outside, the view of Garden City faded into bleak, withered prairie grass, which decorated an endless expanse of flat, undeveloped land as far as the eye could see.

For once, no wind appeared to be blowing, and the dry stalks stood rigidly uneven under a pale, cloudless sky. Nothing about the scenery captured her interest. She'd seen it countless times in her life. The green leather of the seat creaked as she turned to a much more interesting view: her handsome husband, who dozed beside her, their joined hands resting in his lap. A lock of shining black hair had fallen loose over his forehead, and Kristina smoothed it away with her free hand.

It still astonishes me that such an attractive man not only gave plain little me a second glance, he actually married me. Till death do us part. I love him so much. Her mind wandered from the boring landscape to a memory of the previous morning.

Christmas dawned cold and clear, waking us. We slept so late after the exertions of the previous evening. A naughty grin creased her features and her inside clenched at the memory of so much passion. Upon finding themselves snuggled together nude, desire naturally flared again.

Images played out, superimposed over the stalks of prairie grass. Large, calloused hands caressed her in all her favorite places until she felt as pliant as warm wax. Then he grasped her hips and rolled, trying a new position. She shivered at the memory. *How lovely it felt.*

It didn't take long, perched on top of Cody like that, to find completion. It felt so natural just to tell him she loved him. And then... a thrill of warmth shot through her belly at the memory.

The look he gave me told me everything I needed to know. If he hadn't... hadn't achieved his release at that moment, I know he would have responded in kind. I can't imagine a better Christmas present than the knowledge that my husband loves me.

She turned away from the window again, studying his face. A tender smile creased her features.

Cody shifted in his sleep, his head coming to rest on Kristina's shoulder, his hand releasing hers to slide around her waist. She leaned her cheek against his hair, letting her own eyes drift shut.

A violent jolt awakened the couple. *The train's stopping, but how can it be? We're hours from Wichita.*

The sunlight streaming in the window showed Kristina it was still morning. She couldn't have been asleep for more than a few minutes. There was another jolt and from across the carriage, a female voice yelped, and a baby began to cry. Then, to Kristina's horror, a gang of armed men, bandanas covering their faces, stormed into the car, shouting and waving their weapons.

Someone screamed. Kristina shrank back against the window, clutching Cody's hand.

"Give us your valuables and no one gets hurt," the leader shouted in a hoarse, rasping voice. He adjusted his black felt hat low on his head. "Boys, round up the loot."

A skinny assailant in a dirty tan jacket approached one of the seats nearer the front of the car. Over the low back, Kristina could just see a mass of messy brown hair.

"Give me that ring," a voice snarled. The woman squealed, and the man lifted her from the seat, making her screech.

"Shut up," he hollered, slapping her. The blow knocked the poor woman's head sideways.

"Please," she whimpered, "please don't..." and then her voice trailed off. He raised his hand to hit her again and she relented, relaxing her hand so he could wrench a thin gold band from her ring finger. He dropped her back to the seat without another word and moved on.

"Kristina," Cody murmured under his breath, "don't fight over your ring. Give it up."

"But Cody..."

"No. I won't have you hurt. It's just a ring, darlin'."

"Cody, they're not going to let any of us live."

He turned to look deep into her eyes. "I know. But cooperating might buy us some time to come up with a plan."

"Cody, look around. You're the only able-bodied man here. The rest of us are women, children and an elderly couple. How can we possibly take on these armed bandits and succeed?"

"With God, all things are possible, Kristina. Give him the ring."

She closed her eyes, trying to hold back the tears, and tugged the pretty moonstone from her finger. After less than a week of marriage, she already felt naked without it.

A tall stocky bandit with a gray-eyed glare appeared in front of them. Kristina jumped.

"Give it up, folks, and no one gets hurt."

Odd. There's something familiar about the voice. Where have I heard it before? She peeked around the shield of Cody's body but could not learn anything further. The handkerchief over his mouth concealed his features.

Her husband extended his wallet and the ring.

"That's all?" the bandit asked, disgusted. "Who travels with so little money?'

"I'm a pastor," Cody replied, his voice surprisingly calm. "Look, man. I've given you everything I have. Please don't hurt my wife. Promise me."

"Wife." The man looked directly at Kristina for the first time, and he reacted with a violent start. He stalked away without another word, but the way he moved told Kristina everything she needed to know. Sobs clogged her throat, and her eyes burned.

It only took a few minutes for the villains to collect all the valuables in the train car.

"Okay," rasped the leader. "No funny business. Everyone up front, NOW!"

As the passengers obeyed, the robbers gathered near the door.

"On to the next one. Heitschmidt, stay here and guard this lot. We'll go check the other cars."

The stocky man protested softly, too softly for Kristina to overhear the words. A raised fist and a snarl overruled his objection and the other five men left.

The robber stood near the door, blocking the exit, keeping his eyes on the back. There would be no escaping his gaze. He stuck one thumb in his belt loop and leaned against the wall, his glare daring anyone to try something funny. His free hand rested on his pistol.

Kristina took several slow deep breaths. Only once in her life before had she heard the still, small voice of the Lord whisper to her. Today she heard it again and she knew what she had to do. As to the outcome, she had no clue. Only the command was clear.

"Cody," she breathed in her husband's ear, "I have an idea."

He turned to face her. "Kristina..."

"Trust me. Please, honey, you have to listen."

He nodded.

"I'm going to go up there and talk to him. While I keep him busy, get these others out of here." She nodded to their fellow prisoners.

Across from them, a plump, brown-haired matron struggled to keep three small children calm while jiggling a fretful infant. One row behind, the woman who hadn't wanted to give up her ring wept, clutching a hugely swollen belly. Across from her, an elderly couple huddled together. They looked to be over seventy.

"Darlin', if you think I'm going to let you—no! That's foolish, Kristina. Why would I let you go to him? I'll distract him; you get the others out."

"He'll kill you, Cody. I can't let him kill you. Get them out and go get help."

"What makes you think he won't kill you... or worse? These are dangerous men!"

"I know he'll never hurt me." She gulped, trying to contain the sob, but when she spoke again, her voice trembled and broke. "He's... he's my brother."

Cody wrapped his arms around his wife, holding her close. "Are you sure?"

She nodded. "I know his voice, his walk, and the boss called him Heitschmidt. How many of us can there be?"

Cody blinked. "Guess I didn't notice. I was thinking about you." He pulled back and looked into his wife's eyes. She could see he still didn't like the plan but could formulate no other. Pure blazing emotion flared in his beautiful eyes. "I love you, Kristina," he said fiercely. "I've loved you all along. I'm sorry I didn't say so sooner."

"I know, Cody. I've known from the beginning. You didn't have to say anything. And I love you too."

They crushed each other in a powerful embrace. *This is a desperate plan, but what else can we do? These poor people need our help.* Cody kissed her hard on the mouth, squeezed her hand tight, and allowed her to slip past him into the aisle.

She approached the robber with quiet footsteps. His attention seemed to be diverted by something on the blighted Kansas winter landscape outside, so she drew quite close before he noticed her.

"Stay back, miss," he said, his hand going to his gun.

"Calvin?" She made her voice as soft and hesitant as she could.

"No ma'am," the villain replied, but his tone and the guilty shift of his eyes spoke to the lie.

"Yes, it is. Did you think I wouldn't know my own brother?" She kept moving forward until she stood close enough to touch. Grasping the navy handkerchief, she pulled, revealing the face she'd known her whole life.

She stared. She'd known it was him, but seeing him here with the criminals, holding a gun on innocent people, proved to be more than she could bear. The emotions she'd been struggling to suppress spilled over in a flood of burning tears.

"Why, Cal?" she choked.

He didn't pretend to misunderstand. "It's hard to make a fortune at honest work."

"So rather than work hard and be honest, you became a robber? A killer?"

"I haven't killed anyone, Kristina."

She shook her head. "You're with them. You're just as guilty as if you pulled the trigger."

She moved to the side, sinking heavily into the nearest seat and burying her face in her hands. Through the crack in her fingers, she could see him fumbling in his pockets. With his attention diverted, she gave a quick jerk of her head, then returned her focus to Calvin.

To keep him distracted, and cover the sounds of soft, stealthy footsteps moving down the aisle towards the back of the train car, she burst into noisy sobs. As she had hoped, he sank into the seat across the aisle from her and handed her a grubby handkerchief. She dabbed at her eyes.

"What are you doing here, Kris?" he asked her. "I didn't think you traveled anymore."

"I'm on my honeymoon," she whimpered.

"So, you did get married, did you? That fellow said..."

"My husband. Cody Williams. He's the new pastor."

She glanced at her brother, taking in his stricken expression. "You should let us go; let them all go. The poor pregnant lady, the mother with the kids, the old folks. What did they do to deserve this?"

"Life's hard, Kristina. Everyone suffers. Fire, earthquake, train robbery, what's the difference?"

She raised her tear-stained face and glared at him, crossing the aisle and sinking into the seat beside him to grasp his lapel in her fist. "The difference is the choice. Fires and earthquakes just happen. Robberies are done to people by other people. You chose to be part of this gang. You chose to rob this train. You can choose to let them go."

"The boss will never agree, Kristina," he replied sadly. "He doesn't listen to me, I'm the new kid. I've only been with them a short time. I might be able to convince them to spare you since you're my sister, but the others..."

"What will happen to them, Calvin?"

"The boss said no witnesses."

I so hoped I was wrong. "And Cody?"

He shook his head.

This time, genuine sobs overwhelmed her. "I don't want to live without him! I love him, Cal. We've only been married a week!"

Calvin cursed under his breath. "I'm sorry, Kris. If I'd guessed you'd be here..."

"What difference does it make?" she shrieked. "Every person here is someone's sister or brother or husband. What about the little kids? What about the pregnant lady?"

"Calm down, sis. Don't scream. You don't want to attract their attention back here sooner. Listen, there's nothing I can do but try to talk to the boss. Why don't you go back and... sit with your husband? Don't waste time."

Kristina's tears increased until she could neither move nor speak. Calvin hugged her awkwardly. She heard a soft sound as the back door of the car eased open a crack, and hid the noise with a loud, sniffling snort.

How long she sat sobbing next to her brother, Kristina wasn't sure, but just as she was beginning to get ahold of herself, she was plucked into a warm familiar embrace.

Cody. She turned in his arms. "What are you doing here, honey? I thought you were going to get help. Where are the others?"

"Safe," he replied, the warm tone of his voice oozing over her like sun-sweet honey. "But I won't leave without you."

"What did you say?" Calvin faced them, his eyes narrowed, his voice a dangerous hiss. His eyes shot around the now empty train car. "You...argh!" he growled. "What did you do that for?"

"I had to," Cody replied calmly. "What kind of man stands by and lets women and children be slaughtered?"

"They're gonna kill me," Calvin whined. It struck Kristina how young he sounded. And in fact, his twenty-first birthday wouldn't be for a couple of months.

"Then come away with us," she urged. "Give up this criminal life and come home."

"And do what?" he asked.

"Work with Dad at the mercantile. I know he misses you, and Allison just got married, so she won't be able to help out there anymore."

"Allison too?" A strange look passed over Calvin's features, reminding his sister he'd been mooning over the pretty blond for many years.

She ignored the question. "Please, Cal. Let's just go. All of us, quickly, while the others are distracted."

He thought for a moment, affection for his sister warring with loyalty to his gang. At last, he shook his head. "I can't. I know who they are, they'll come and hunt me down. Besides, like you said, I'm just as guilty as the ones who pulled the trigger. If the gang doesn't kill me, I'll be hanged."

"Wonderful," Cody said, sarcasm dripping from his ever-deepening drawl, "you're willing to sign your sister's death warrant to save your own hide. Are you sure you're a Heitschmidt? That's not what the family I know would do."

"Oh, shut up," Calvin sulked.

"I won't," Cody replied. "You're a young fool. Stop playing robber and let us off this train. Blast it, man. She's your sister! Just look how frightened she is."

His firm voice and harsh words captured Calvin's attention. He turned his face toward Kristina and opened his mouth to speak...

"Fulton, I need your help. Lock up the bank and come with me. We're forming a posse." Sheriff Brody stepped into the room where Wesley sat at his desk, counting deposits. His boots clunked noisily on the wood planks of the floor.

"What happened?" Wesley glanced up from his record book.

"There's a train robbery in progress. Young Will Watson just rode in on a horse three times too big for him. His mother and brothers and some other people are hiding in an abandoned farmstead a few miles down the tracks. He said there were other people still on the train. If we can catch the gang..."

Wes nodded. "Just a minute. I need to let my wife know..." But there was no need. Allison flew into the bank, little Melissa clutched in her arms.

"Wes, did you hear about the... Oh, Sheriff. Thank God! You have to go, Wes. You have to!"

"Calm down, Allie. What's going on?" He'd expected she would protest him going on such a dangerous excursion.

"Kristina and Cody are on that train!"

Without another word, Wesley pulled on his heavy coat, kissed his wife and daughter, and ran for the door, Sheriff Brody close on his heels.

What Calvin would have said, Cody never knew. At that moment, the gang burst back into the car, whooping and shouting. Apparently, the other cars had been more lucrative than this one. The boss held a bulging flour sack in one hand and was waving his gun in the air in triumph. Kristina shrank against her husband, and he pushed her behind his back.

"Okay, Heitschmidt, let's clean up this group and get the hell out of here."

Cody gulped. His words didn't bode well for the passengers in the other cars.

"Listen, boss," Calvin said softly, "this is my sister and her husband. We don't have to kill them, do we? Can't we just let them go? I mean, he's a preacher. You don't want a preacher on your conscience, do you?"

The boss shrugged. Clearly, neither sister nor preacher meant anything to him. "Heitschmidt, you're soft. After all we done, one preacher ain't going make any difference." He glanced at Kristina and something ugly flashed in his eyes. "Sister, eh? She's a bit pretty. Maybe we can take her back to the compound, she might be fun to have around. What do you say, girly girl? Would you like to come back with us?"

Kristina gagged, pressing closer to Cody's back. "Not a chance in hell," she gritted out.

The boss shrugged again. "Too bad." He pointed his gun at the two of them.

"Please," Cody said. "Please don't hurt my wife."

"Sorry, preacher," the boss replied. "Nothing personal, but she looks too clever. Can't have her identifying us."

Cody offered a quick prayer. He retreated a step, pushing Kristina behind him, away from the criminals, intending to make a desperate, hopeless run for the back exit of the train car.

He whirled. Behind him, the click of a pistol being cocked echoed through the room. He didn't look. He couldn't.

"I love you, Kristina," he said softly. He wanted those to be the last words he said, the last she heard.

"I love you," she replied, her voice breaking. She slipped her hand into his.

The pistol roared, and Kristina screamed. The sound of the shot seemed to echo again and again. *Funny, there's no pain, and I'm still standing.* Cody looked down at his uninjured body. *How could the boss have missed from such close range?*

The sound of gunshots reverberated in the train car, far longer than a structure so small ought to be able to echo. Cody risked a glance at the window to see a welcome vision. A crowd of men on horseback, led by Sheriff Brody's familiar dark-mustached face raced towards them, pistols firing. Deputy Wade brought up the rear, driving a wagon filled with more townsfolk.

The gang poured out of the train car to engage the posse.

But what happened? Where's the boss? Why weren't we killed? He turned back to the spot and his jaw dropped in astonishment. The villain lay prone on the floor, bleeding from a hole in the middle of his hat. Calvin stood over him, a wisp of smoke protruding from the muzzle of his pistol.

Only one bandit remained, staring in open-mouthed shock at the young trainee who had suddenly turned on them.

"Threaten my sister?" Calvin growled. "Not on my watch."

"Heitschmidt," the other bandit stammered, "you shot the boss! What the hell were you thinking?"

"Did you hear what he said? No one's going to do... *that* to Kristina. No way."

The other man didn't reply. His gaze went from the corpse to the young man before him and back before he reached for his pistol.

Without pausing for reflection, Cody rushed him. The odds of escaping a gang of armed men had been slim. But two men— one with a gun —should be able to take down a single assailant, allowing Kristina to escape unharmed.

The robber's gun flew out of its holster before Cody could even take two steps towards him.

Diving low, he took the man's legs out from under him as Calvin raised his pistol and aimed. The roar of the two weapons in the enclosed metal structure temporarily obliterated Cody's hearing. Time seemed to slow as he tackled the wriggling bandit to the floor, pinning him. One shoulder stayed trapped easily. The other was slippery and difficult to hold. Cody pushed harder.

As his hearing slowly returned, the first sound to register on his senses was a female scream. *Kristina.* He turned to look at his wife. She stood, pale but blessedly uninjured, holding onto one wrought-iron armrest for support. Next, he heard an agonized groan. Glancing down, he saw blood pouring from a wound in the criminal's shoulder, a wound he was grinding into the floor with the heel of his hand.

The man tried to move, and Cody saw a black metal object in his hand. *He still has his gun, and he's trying to aim it.*

Movement stirred behind him. He pressed harder on the injury, hoping to distract the man. Long fingers dotted with freckles yanked the pistol from the man's hand and cocked it, pointing it past Cody. "Stop fighting." Her hands shook, but her voice sounded calm.

The man continued to squirm, trying to shove Cody off him. Cody lifted him by both shoulders and slammed his head down onto the iron plate beneath them. The criminal released a startled *Oof,* and his flailing limbs fell limp. His eyes rolled back.

Cody took the opportunity to strip off his belt and restrain the fellow by binding his arms.

The task complete, he rose and turned to his wife, plucking the gun from her hands. She stepped over the bandit's prone body and thrust herself into his arms. He crushed her in a powerful hug. *Thank God. We're alive and miraculously unharmed.*

A strange gurgling sound captured their attention, and they turned as one, horrified to see Calvin laid out on the floor, a gaping hole in his belly, thick blood oozing out to pool on the floor around him.

Kristina wrenched herself out of her husband's embrace and flew to her brother's side, crouching over him and taking his hand in hers.

"Kris," he muttered.

"Hush, Cal, don't try to talk. We'll get you help."

"Too late," he choked, and Cody knew it was true. A bullet to the gut was not a survivable injury. "I'm done, sis." He coughed, and pink-tinged foam collected in the corner of his mouth. "I'm sorry. Tell Dad. Sorry."

"No, Cal. I won't tell him that, I'll tell him the truth. I'll tell him you're a hero, that you died to save me." Her voice broke.

A hint of a smile appeared on the wounded man's lips.

Cody approached, kneeling beside his wife, sliding his arm around her shoulders.

"Will you say a prayer for me, preacher?" Calvin asked. His voice was growing very faint. "Won't do any good." He gagged, choked. "I done too much. Can't be forgiven. But it might make my sister feel better."

"You're wrong," Cody told him calmly. "Jesus forgave the soldiers who crucified him. He invited the thief on the cross beside him into heaven. I know you grew up in the church, Calvin. Don't you remember the scriptures? 'Anyone who calls on the name of the Lord will be saved.'"

"I wanted to make amends. Thought I had time."

"You do. Pray with me, Calvin. Repent."

Calvin gagged again. An agonized groan emerged. Kristina grasped her brother's hand tighter. Cody could see her knuckles turning white, but poor Calvin was beyond caring.

He led his brother-in-law in a brief prayer of repentance. By the end, Calvin gasped each word, struggling to draw breath into his lungs. *He has moments, no more.*

"Calvin," Cody said, "the scriptures say if we confess, God

will forgive. You confessed. You are forgiven. Go in peace, brother."

The young man's next exhalation was an unearthly rattle, and then his heaving chest went still.

His task complete, Cody gently closed his staring eyes and extricated his wife's hand from that of the corpse. Silent tears streamed down Kristina's face. Cody circled Calvin's body and enfolded her in his arms. She laid her face against his shoulder and wept. With one toe, Cody nudged the bandana away from Calvin, so it lay under the shoulder of the dead robber boss. He wouldn't lie, but with luck, he wouldn't have to.

A moment later, Wesley Fulton burst into the train car, a shotgun cradled in his arm. He looked over the devastation with an expression of deep disgust. "Am I ever glad to see you two are all right. My wife would have my hide if I came home without you," he quipped. Then his eyes fell on the nearest body. "Calvin Heitschmidt!" he exclaimed. "What the hell is he doing here? Oh, uh, sorry, Cody."

"I'm not going to complain, Wesley. This situation is rather extreme."

Sheriff Dylan Brody stomped up onto the train, muttering under his breath. "Oh," he said, startled to see them. "I'm so glad you two are all right. And... did you catch one of them?" He waved at the unconscious bandit whose chest rose and fell in rattling snores. "That's better than we did."

"What, they got away?" Cody's teeth ground together.

"Yeah, we killed one, but the other two escaped. Unfortunately, we lost Deputy Charles as well. What on earth went on here?"

"Well," Cody replied slowly, grieving inside at the thought of officiating a funeral for the young father with so many children, "you can imagine how it started. Scary men with guns. Yelling. We managed to get the other passengers off the train, and then, well, Kristina's brother turned up, and between us, we managed to take down these two."

"The other passengers are alive?" The sheriff suddenly looked like Christmas morning had arrived all over again.

"Yes," Cody replied. Kristina shook harder than ever and he stroked her back. "There were only a few in our car, but we got them away before things turned too ugly. Oh, that reminds me..." He passed Kristina to Wesley and yanked the bag of loot out from under the boss's body. A quick rummage produced the gold and moonstone ring, which he tucked into his pocket.

He also found the thin band which had been taken from the pregnant woman. He handed it to Brody. "Sheriff, this belonged to a young woman who objected strongly to losing it. Can you please be sure it gets back to her?"

Dylan accepted the ring as Cody continued. "What about the passengers in the other cars?"

The sheriff gave a grim shake of his head as he accepted the ring.

"None?" Kristina gasped. She swallowed convulsively.

Sensing an imminent crisis, Cody led her outside. Kristina crashed to her knees on the dry, crackling prairie grass and vomited. He waited nearby and handed her his handkerchief when she staggered back towards him.

"Dylan, could I take Cody and Kristina home now?" Wesley urged. "They've been through enough."

"Wait," Cody interjected. "First let's round up the other survivors. They can come too. It'll be a tight fit in the wagon, but we'll manage. They've suffered as much as we have."

It only took a few minutes to retrieve the others from the abandoned farmstead where they'd been hiding. In a few minutes, Dylan had bundled them all onto the wagon. Cody sat against one side of the open, straw-lined bed and pulled Kristina into his lap. At the moment, he didn't care in the slightest about propriety. She snuggled against his chest, her face buried in his shoulder while he stroked her back.

Next to them, the pregnant woman clutched her wedding

ring to her heart with one hand, pressing the other to her belly. Tears streamed down her cheeks.

The sight reminded Cody of his own wife's loss. He fished in his pocket until he found Kristina's ring and slipped it back onto her finger.

Her gaze met his. "I love you, Cody," she told him, her heart in her eyes, emotion bleeding from every pore.

"I love you, darlin'," he replied, hugging her closer. Then the wagon lurched into motion, carrying the bedraggled and traumatized survivors towards safety and home.

About the Author

In the world of the written word, Simone Beaudelaire strives for technical excellence while advancing a worldview in which the sacred and the sensual blend into stories of people whose relationships are founded in faith but are no less passionate for it. Unapologetically explicit, yet undeniably classy, Beaudelaire's 20+ novels aim to make readers think, cry, pray... and get a little hot and bothered.

In real life, the author's alter-ego teaches composition at a community college in a small western Kansas town, where she lives with her four children, three cats, and husband—fellow author Edwin Stark.

As both romance writer and academic, Beaudelaire devotes herself to promoting the rhetorical value of romance in hopes of overcoming the stigma associated with literature's biggest female-centered genre.

To learn more about Simone Beaudelaire and discover more Next Chapter authors, visit our website at www.nextchapter.pub.

Books by Simone Beaudelaire

High Plains Holiday
ISBN: 978-4-91055-778-6

Published by
Next Chapter
2-5-6 SANNO
SANNO BRIDGE
143-0023 Ota-Ku, Tokyo
+818035793528

19th May 2022

Lightning Source UK Ltd.
Milton Keynes UK
UKHW010202070223
416581UK00004B/257